Pocklington stared in disbelief at the cavorting figures in the swirling autumnal mist, tiny human caricatures fashioned out of straw, evilly mocking him.

It was just a sick joke, he tried to convince himself. Kids from the village had come up here, made some corn puppets, were somehow working them whilst hidden in the rapidly thickening mist.

It did not ring true. These effigies were all too real, living malevolent entities. The creatures began to laugh, shrill titterings that escalated to high-pitched shrieks as they embarked upon some kind of frenzied death dance.

His vision started to darken, mercifully spared him the sight of his impish attackers closing in on him. He screamed, knew that he would be just one more unexplained death in a growing list of recent victims.

also by Guy N. Smith

The Busker

Guy N. Smith

Bulldog Books
A Division of Black Hill Books

Bulldog Books
A Division of Black Hill Books

A Bulldog paperback original 1998
Copyright © Guy N. Smith 1998

Shortlisted for the Lichfield Prize

ISBN 0 9532701 0 6

Typesetting by Hal C. F. Astell, Halifax

Cover illustration by Andrew Compton

For Laurence and Liz James, a longtime friendship that has meant so much. Long may it continue.

The publishers would like to thank
Hal C. F. Astell, Andrew Compton,
Ralph James of James Redshaw Ltd,
Lichfield, and Nancy Webber for their
invaluable help and support.

Part One
Summer

CHAPTER ONE

Fiona Deeps was uneasy. She had awoken with an inexplicable nagging tension that had persisted as the morning progressed like one of those niggling headaches which were destined to remain throughout the day. There was no logical reason for it, she attempted to convince herself. In vain she tried to stop fidgeting, re-arranging the floral display in the hallway until she had run out of permutations. Maybe it was due to the weather. No, it wasn't, the sun had shone continuously for seven weeks now and if the farmers were crying out for rain then that was their misfortune.

In which case it was all John's fault. Most things were. She wrinkled her forehead and tightened her lips at the thought of her husband. Tall and balding, you took him for fifty when he was still only an ageing forty-two. An agrochemist, his appointment on to the board of directors necessitated his wearing an expensively tailored suit at all times. His idea of casual wear was what most men wore to the office and their recent move into village life wouldn't change him one iota. Work was his hobby; he invariably brought a bulging briefcase home in the evenings. The last two weekends had been spent at conferences at the National Exhibition Centre. She had no worries about his having a mistress, he wouldn't have the time. Nor the inclination. She had become used to his frequent absences from home coupled with his hermit-like existence in the new office extension on the gable end of the house. Don't disturb me, I've got work to do. He always had and he always would have. It was beginning to eat into her. She was under stress, that was the root of her problem.

'Don't pester, darling!' Fiona snapped as she caught Sharon's reflection in the hall mirror. Their fifteen-year-old daughter bore a striking resemblance to herself: shoulder length raven hair, attractive features that were marred by an expression of discontent, frustration that led to a tantrum if she could not have her own way. There was an impatience about the teenager in the very way she descended the stairs.

'I thought we were going shopping, Mother?'

'Yes, darling, we are. Shortly. When I'm ready.'

'I'm ready.'

'Well, I'm not.' Fiona turned away, tried to think of something else to

11

do, on principle.

'What have you got to do?' A challenge, head-on, the girl swinging her handbag against the stair rail like a pendulum. The repetitive *thump-thump* made Fiona want to yell at her.

Fiona took a deep breath, let it out slowly. 'I've got to dry the breakfast things.'

'They'll drip dry.'

'I *like* to dry them.'

'I'll see to it for you. You get the car out.'

Fiona watched her daughter go through to the kitchen. Damn her, she wouldn't dry up a plate any other time. Anything she did was geared to suit herself, the selfish little cow. John had made her that way, set the example all along. GCSEs are more important than household chores, work comes first. It's the housewife whose duty it is to be in the kitchen, no one else. Male chauvinism rubbing off on your daughter.

Fiona went out through the front door, slammed it behind her. The bright sunlight dazzled her, hurt her eyes for a few seconds. She stood there waiting for the feeling to pass, saw the neatly mown lawns, the shrubberies, the weedless gravelled drive that wound its way down to the road. Immaculate in every respect, like the half-timbered house. John took the credit because he earned the money to pay a gardener and handyman. But he wouldn't fork out for somebody to come in to do the cooking and cleaning. No way, that was his wife's duty.

That sense of unease was stronger now, had her mentally recoiling. *As if something awful was destined to happen today.* Like a road accident on the way into Lichfield, or perhaps just a scrape and a bump in the car park. Or her handbag snatched. She felt the dampness of perspiration on her forehead. It was Friday, but not the thirteenth. Don't be so damnably stupid! You're just overwrought, thanks to John and now Sharon. Between them they were getting her down. Maybe she should go away for a few days, a cooling off period, leave them to it and see how they coped. No, the place would be in a dreadful mess when she returned. See the doctor then, go on a course of relaxants. That wasn't the answer, either. There wasn't one, at least none that she could think of.

'Is something wrong, Mother?'

Fiona tensed, resisted the temptation to scream, 'Yes, you and your father, that's what's wrong.' Instead, she walked slowly, slightly unsteadily, towards the open doors of the double garage where the Justy stood, filmed with dust. John had told her before he left to get it washed. She would call in at the garage on the London Road and put it through the car wash. Because, ultimately, she always did as she was told. That was her problem.

She took her time. Deliberately. Sharon could damned well wait, whether she liked it or not. She didn't like it; Fiona would have been disappointed if her daughter had not sighed, clicked her tongue and paced up and down.

The car refused to start, the engine whining, firing once and then cutting out. Fiona waited, feigning the patience which she did not possess, watching her daughter in the rear view mirror and secretly savouring the other's frustration. The girl's make-up was outrageous. She was far too young to daub herself with mascara; she looked a tart. Fiona had objected at the outset but John had overruled her, not because he favoured cosmetics on a fifteen-year-old but simply because he wanted to avoid a row which would distract him from his work. Sharon had gloated, was pushing her mother to the brink of her stretched endurance.

The Justy fired again, held this time. Fiona revved, mentally directed the exhaust fumes in Sharon's direction and reversed out into the drive. Sharon got in, slammed the passenger door and vibrated Fiona's nerves.

Something awful was going to happen today, she was sure of it.

Neither of them spoke as Fiona edged the car out into the lane, watched the mirror on the gate pillar, tensed in anticipation of screeching brakes and squealing tyres. But there was no other vehicle in sight.

Fiona's weekly trip into the city was going to be severely disrupted even if nothing worse happened. On principle, her daughter would not accompany her round the market, share the hassle of food shopping in the supermarket. She might or might not join her for lunch in the art centre restaurant. Oh, no, it would be more fraught than that. Sharon would go off on her own and would not arrive back in the Minster car park until at least twenty minutes after the agreed meeting time. Again, on teenage principle. Neither of them would speak on the return journey and probably not for some time after they arrived home. A deliberately contrived unpleasant atmosphere. Maybe that was the reason for Fiona's apprehension. It had probably been weighing on her subconscious throughout the nocturnal hours.

August was a depressing month, anyway, Fiona decided. Usually it was wet; this year was an exception. Summer's last fling. You were edging into autumn and winter was only a step away. The last few winters, when the Deeps family had been living in Sutton Coldfield, had been mild. Now that they had, or rather John had, decided upon a move to a more rural area, the pattern would change. Blizzards and snowdrifts that even a four-wheel-drive Justy would be unable to overcome. John would stay in town, the school would close and Sharon would be home with her mother, and teenage neurosis would step up a gear.

There was a traffic snarl-up, roadworks where the signals appeared

13

not to be synchronized. Sharon let out another sigh, crossed and uncrossed her feet. Fiona hoped that her own posture was one of total relaxation. They were deliberately needling each other.

Fiona drove twice round the car park before she found an empty space. Sharon was already depressing the door lever.

'Hold on.' Fiona's tone was terse. 'We'd better make some arrangements for meeting up.'

'I'll see you back here, Mother.'

'Lunch?'

'I *might* eat at Kim's.' An element of uncertainty in case her mother decided to check up on her, combined with a tilt at middle-class eating establishments. 'I'll see you back here.'

'All right. Quarter to two and don't be late.'

The door slammed and Sharon was gone. Fiona allowed herself a few moments of relief before that uneasiness came surging back. She had felt this way when those soldiers had been gunned down by terrorists on the station the day she and John had come into Lichfield to view their present house. That had been a Friday, too. Oh, God!

As she locked the car up, another frightening, illogical thought hit her with the force of a physical blow, had her steadying herself up against the door. *Maybe that awful unknown something which she had been dreading had already happened.*

Again, she tried to tell herself that it was all in the mind, but she was shaking visibly as she headed across towards the narrow passageway that led through to Bird Street. There was no sign of Sharon; she had gone wherever she was going. And Fiona reflected that, had it not been for the fact that she was obliged to wait for her daughter's return in approximately two hours' time, she would have got back in the car and driven home, and whatever Friday had in store for her could have waited until Saturday. Now she found herself trapped in an aura of impending doom.

It was as though time had ceased to exist, and Fiona was caught up in a void where life went on as before but nobody got anywhere. Long queues at the supermarket checkouts, harassed mothers attempting to control young children but giving up in the end and allowing them to run about and scream, cashiers who either ignored customers or showed irritation at loaded trolleys. It seemed that everybody was paying by cheque and having difficulty in writing them out.

'Next, please!'

Fiona started, trembled. The checkout girl grabbed impatiently for her trolley, began ringing up the items. It was as though everybody was talking but nobody was listening.

The shopping was stacked in the boot of the Justy, plastic carrier bags that slid and bulged, spilled out anything that rolled. Fiona's thoughts turned to lunch; she wasn't hungry but at least there was company in the Garrick Café. A kind of sanctuary, a cocoon that would protect her from her indeterminable terror, a backwater away from home and the hostile outside world.

It didn't work out that way. The art college was closed for the summer holidays so those with whom Fiona socialized on a casual Friday lunchtime basis were absent. The place was full of noisy strangers, as if those mothers from the supermarket had also sought refuge in here and brought their screaming children with them.

Fiona ate a pizza and two salads, didn't bother with a sweet. A couple of youngsters were squabbling and nobody tried to stop them. Even the ducks on the pool outside were quarrelsome; it was as if her own feeling of unease had enveloped the city, had affected the birds, too. She shuddered. If whatever it was had already happened then she was terrified of discovering what it was.

She was back at the car at one forty, tensely optimistic.

Maybe just this once Sharon would show up on time. It was damnably hot and Fiona opened both doors, leaned against the driver's. Her mouth was dry, and there was a sour taste on her palate. She waited. When the cathedral clock chimed the quarter hour she jumped, felt her intestines griping. You stupid child, where are you? We have to get away from here. I don't know why but we can't stop here.

Fiona stood there staring across at the cathedral, its three spires reaching right up into the sky, its magnificent architecture marred on the south side by unsightly scaffolding. She recalled the coffee morning at the deanery a few weeks back, wondered idly how much it had raised towards the restoration fund. It didn't matter; all that concerned her was Sharon's safe return.

She almost screamed when the two chimes sounded, clutched the car door with an intensity that whitened her knuckles. The echoes lingered in her tortured brain, throbbed at her temples. Wildly she searched the shoppers meandering back on to the car park but there was no raven-haired teenager walking haughtily amongst them. A policeman stood over by the Dam Street exit, maybe sent here to check on the validity of road fund discs. Mutely she screamed at him: 'Officer, my daughter's missing. I know she's in trouble. Maybe mugged, raped. . . *murdered*'.

A wave of nausea hit her, her vision blurring, darkening with red streaks until she threw off the feeling of faintness forcibly. If she collapsed they would take her to hospital and then Sharon would be at the mercy of. . .

Somehow she managed to walk, leaving the car open and unguarded, heading back towards the passageway that was a short cut to the city centre. That was the way Sharon would come. Maybe she was still in Kim's Kabin, being chatted up by undesirable youths. Somehow the teenager's rebellious nature attracted the worst amongst boyfriends, challenged society and her parents in the most hurtful way possible. She would grow out of it, it was just a phase she was going through, searching the lower echelons of the class system for companionship, resenting the fact that her father was a director of. . . Sharon, please be safe and we'll forgive you. Blast John, it was all his fault. If he spent more time with his daughter. . .

'Sharon!' Fiona's cry of euphoria and relief died as suddenly as it had begun, hopelessness but not embarrassment in her expression as the dark-haired girl walking in front of her turned sharply, looked round in surprise, quickened her step.

I know something has happened to her already. I know!

It was as she emerged on to the pavement in front of Woolworths that Fiona heard the music. It came at her through the hubbub of shoppers' voices; even the constant roar of city centre traffic was unable to drown it. Haunting, lilting, weird and wonderful in its own way, penetrating her agonized train of thought so that even Sharon was temporarily forgotten. Mournful and yet exhilarating, quickening her step and seeming to draw her towards the cobbled market square and its array of stalls over which Johnson's statue towered, his carved features pensive as though even he was forced to listen.

It came from nowhere in particular yet was everywhere, the strains of a harmonica that were both soft and piercing, notes so perfect that subconsciously you marvelled at a melody that was strange and yet familiar; urging you on, hastening your pace so that you bumped into passers-by, pushed rudely past them.

Traders and shoppers seemed unaware of the music, but there was a small crowd huddled around the plinth of the statue, pressing eagerly forward, oblivious of all else except that which commanded their attention like the ancient mariner at the wedding feast. Youths and children fascinated by some street musician, seemingly spellbound rather than idling to listen, crowding the unseen busker, the throng growing even as Fiona hurried to join them, toddlers who had slipped from their mother's watchful eye as she purchased from a stall, teenagers with forgotten drink cans in their hands, their bodies beginning to sway softly to the rhythm.

Fiona stiffened. She didn't want to go any nearer. The last thing she wanted was to look upon whoever was playing that compelling music. It was just some wandering musician, probably a hippy, a dropout living off social security and earning an illicit few pounds on the side. There was a law against that; buskers required a licence to play in public. He was cheating the system. She tried to turn away, intending to walk through the avenue of market stalls and into the adjacent street, check that trendy café to see if Sharon was there. She had to be, she must be.

But for some inexplicable, frightening reason Fiona's feet moved in the direction of the gathering beneath the statue. She tried to stop them, willed herself to turn back, but it was futile. It was as though she had no control over her feet, which moved with an unsteady determination of their own towards the crowd of youngsters. And all the time that eerie music was becoming louder. And louder.

She found herself on the fringe of the listeners, a lone adult amongst children and adolescents, pressing up against them as she peered over and between bodies in an attempt to view the mysterious player. No heads turned in her direction, every one of them was staring intently at the strange ragbag figure who sat with his back up against the plinth playing a long, dented and scratched harmonica.

He was dressed in crumpled, filthy khaki denims, probably throwouts from some foreign armed services, the kind sold by the thousand in a multitude of ex-WD surplus stores. Torn and stained with grease and dirt, they hung from his near-skeletal figure. A green and brown camouflage hat was pushed back on his shock of unruly black hair but it was his features that brought an intake of breath, a gasp of amazement. There was the stamp of aristocracy on his finely moulded features, an expression of gentleness in those flashing dark eyes that roved his audience. With his long beard straggling down on to his chest, Fiona had the impression that this man might have stepped right out of some stained glass church window or maybe a seventeenth-century oil painting, some divine power granting him three-dimensional life.

The melody vibrated her brain like some catchy tune that you heard on the radio, knowing even at the time that you would be unable to get it out of your head for days, pleasant at the outset but eventually becoming an irritant so that you fought in vain to dispel it. You hummed with it as though it was familiar, would have put words to it had you known them. Everybody was swaying gently to the rhythm, oblivious of all else.

Those dark eyes found her own, smiled. She knew that she smiled back, nodded her unwilling approval, entered into a kind of affinity with this musician whom she had never seen before. She wanted to be angry but it was impossible. He was doing no harm. He was entertaining those who otherwise might have roamed the city streets aimlessly, become bent on mischief and vandalism. If he cheated the system then it was excusable, acceptable.

His age was indeterminable. He might have been thirty or forty, classless in his own inimitable way. So gentle and yet. . . icy fingers stroked the base of her spine and a tiny shiver rippled its way up to her neck and on into her scalp. In some strange, illogical way she found him. . . frightening!

It was then that she noticed Sharon, leaning up against the statue base just behind the busker, watching him, listening to him with an intentness that bordered on the hypnotic, oblivious of everything except this stranger and his melody which had her body swaying in time to it.

'Sharon!'

Fiona felt the shriek in her throat but somehow it never left her lips, as though this mystic music had throttled an untimely interruption, silenced the sacrilege before it was born. She wanted to go to her daughter, to drag her away forcibly, but the crowd had swelled, hemmed her in on all sides. She was reminded of some modern day Pied Piper who had lured youngsters from their homes and play for his own insidious purpose.

Why *me*, she asked herself. I'm an adult, all these others are teenagers and children. But there was no answer, only that she, too, was transfixed by the spellbinding tune, a rhythm that speeded and slowed, played with an unbelievable harmony that a battered instrument such as this one had no right to produce.

The busker had stopped, was up on his feet, the harmonica pushed into a pocket of his ragged denims. *Yet the melody continued, never paused, had those listeners still moving in time with it.*

Because it's all in the mind, Fiona wanted to shriek, clutch at her ears in an attempt to shut it out. I'll hear it for ever more, waking or sleeping!

The busker was gone. She had not seen him leave, but somehow he had slipped away through his audience, left them with a reminder of his presence, their brains throbbing in the wake of his playing.

'Sharon!' This time the shout came out, a piercing cry that had the girl opposite stirring as though she had been awoken from a deep sleep, staring across the confused throng, recognizing her own name and wondering who had called her.

'Sharon, come here!' Fiona fought her way through those around her, rushed forward in sudden panic, grabbed her daughter's arm before Sharon, too, disappeared. Oh, thank God! I knew that something awful was going to happen today.

They were back in the car, the doors still open, the key in the ignition. Fiona could not remember the walk back down the litter-strewn alley. That tune was still hammering in her brain, there was no way she could get rid of it. She felt the beginning of a headache; it might attain migraine proportions.

'Darling, are you sure you're all right?' She looked at her daughter

18

anxiously. Sharon was staring straight ahead of her, unseeing eyes glazed.

Sharon nodded, it seemed with an effort. 'I'm OK, thanks.' Subdued, her earlier rebellious attitude was gone, replaced by what appeared to be relief.

'Who. . . who was that man?' Fiona tensed. She did not really want to know. Just another drifter, a hippy out to make a quick buck with his old mouth organ. No, that wasn't right, there was something about him that was so different. So frightening.

'I. . . don't. . . know.' Sharon spoke slowly, falteringly, lapsed back into silence.

Fiona started the engine, reversed out of the parking space. That melody was driving her mad, and her headache was worsening. The sooner they were home the better, away from the city and its mysterious busker who played strange music and left those who heard it with a terrifying reminder of his talents.

CHAPTER TWO

Dick Kirby pandered to his ego for just a couple of minutes. Secretly, almost self-consciously, as he stood there on the crowded pavement on the corner of the market square, he fixed his gaze proudly on the cover of the hardback volume which occupied part of the central display in the bookshop window. It was like looking at a mirror, seeing a minute reflection of himself from a distance. Well built, a neatly trimmed beard, that same red and white checked shirt which he wore now, the only difference being that in the jacket picture he was leaning on a fork with goats and donkeys in the background obligingly trying to screen the dilapidated farm building behind them.

The lines on his weather-beaten features crinkled into a half smile of pride as he read the title of the book twice. Just to make sure. *Traditional Farming Methods*. Beneath it a name, one that caused his pulses to race, his heartbeat step up a gear. *Richard Kirby*. A dream perhaps, a cruel one from which he would be catapulted back to reality, shaken awake by Brenda, his petite fair-haired wife. 'Wake up, Dick, it's after seven, time to be getting up.' Throwing back the bedsheets, groaning at the thought of another routine day of bureaucracy in the council's planning department. But no, it was real enough, his book had made it into print, set his small organic farm apart from those of his more traditional neighbours.

It *was* a dream but it was one that had come true. His ego trip over, he gave a small sigh of relief. A year ago he had been earning his living from a secure but boring nine-till-five job in a stuffy office, getting rid of his aggression in the evenings and at weekends on his thirty acre smallholding. A hobby, it could never be anything else. It was now. He had thrown the jibes of his neighbours right back in their faces, the 'idealistic crank' had proved his point, his book had been featured on both radio and television, his traditional and organic farming methods had become a showpiece on the outskirts of the city, already the public were paying for the privilege of seeing how crops were grown and livestock tended in the days of their grandfathers, albeit in a small way. And this was just the beginning.

Down to earth again, he recalled the meeting with his bank manager just half an hour ago. With cautious confidence the other had given his approval to a £20,000 overdraft. Dick could not have made it without the book. Now he must forsake his typewriter for the shire horse which pulled his plough, concentrate on rearing those rare breeds of pigs and poultry. *Traditional Farming Methods* had been but a springboard to practical success but it had been a pleasant and exciting way of launching his pastime into a commercial venture. He would be forty in a month's time; he told himself yet again that life was about to begin.

It was almost an effort to wrench himself away from that bookshop window. The proprietors had asked him to conduct a signing session next Friday, another brief couple of hours of glory. The *Mercury* was doing a feature on him the same day, good publicity for both his 'open' farm and the book. Then it was back to hard work, enduring all weathers on the land whilst Brenda conducted parties of tourists round. There would be problems, of course, but their quality of life would improve. There would be no pedantic bosses, no regular hours. You worked all hours. For yourself.

Dick checked his watch. Two fifteen. He had to be getting back home. There would be time to repair that piece of wire mesh which the goats had pulled down before picking up Ben, their nine-year-old son, from the friends with whom he had been spending the day.

Slowly, meticulously, savouring again that sense of deep satisfaction, Dick filled and lit his aluminium-stemmed pipe. It was then that he heard the music.

As it penetrated his thoughts he wondered if by chance the fair had returned. No, it only came at Whitsun and for the Bower, so it wasn't that. He turned, stared towards the market stalls, no more than idle curiosity. The canvas awnings screened his view. It seemed to be coming from over by Johnson's statue. A kid with a mouth organ possibly; no, children didn't play like that, they blew, hooted, made harsh sounds. Brenda had bought one for Ben when he was five; Dick had discreetly hidden it somewhere, and it had never come to light again. Even he now could not remember exactly where he had put it.

The shortest route back to the car park was straight on down Dam Street. Instead, he found himself crossing the road towards the market square. Which was silly, because he wasn't really interested enough to find out who was playing that harmonica. Was he? He really should be getting back home.

He pushed his way down an avenue of stalls. This was stupid. He really did not have the time to satisfy an idle whim. There was a crowd gathered round Samuel Johnson's statue, mostly kids with time on their hands. Dick glanced up at the stone effigy, saw the great man himself slumped in his chair. Pensive. He, too, appeared to be listening to this strange music. That was an even crazier notion.

It was the kind of melody that was pleasant at first, Dick decided, but would get on your nerves after a while. You would find yourself humming it, try to shut it out, but discover it lingered on in your brain. It might plague you for days.

The busker was sitting on the plinth, eyes half closed, playing his mouth organ effortlessly. His audience had pushed forward, seemingly spellbound, swaying in time to the gentle rhythm. A ragbag of a hippy, filthy denims that doubtless smelled of sweat and urine, maybe a residue of the peace convoy that had camped up on the Chase during Festival Week.

Dick tried to stop his fingers tapping against his leg, was annoyed because his body wanted to move in time with this weird music. A ballad, probably, some kind of folk music. His eyes roved the listeners; teenagers and young children. He felt self-conscious in case anybody saw him standing there.

A girl leaning against the base of the statue just behind the busker caught his eye, and he recognized a girl from the village, Sharon Deeps. To his relief, the recognition did not appear to be mutual. He wondered what she was doing here.

Well, he supposed it wasn't really surprising. She was much the same as these other adolescents even though she did have wealthy parents and lived in that big house in the village. Her mother had brought her down to the farm a week or two ago to look around. A decade ago he'd have called them typical yuppies, moving out of the city to enjoy country life, waxed jackets, green wellies and a four-wheel-drive which they must take down to the car wash every time it got mud-splattered. She probably didn't even remember him; he was just another country bumpkin to her.

He watched her out of the corner of his eye. She was really into this sort of music, there was no doubt about that; eyes closed as if she was in some kind of trance, bosom heaving as she followed the lilting melody, speeding up, slowing down. Damn it, it was starting to get to him too.

It took a conscious effort to drag himself away. He stumbled on the cobbles and as he stepped into the road a klaxon blared at him and a car brushed his clothing. He started, found that he was trembling. Hell, he could have walked right out in front of that Mini! He told himself it was just sheer carelessness, that it was nothing to do with the harmonica music which followed him all the way back to where the Land Rover was parked. And even then it refused to leave him in peace.

It was much later than Dick realized when he drove the Land Rover into the small farmyard. Even allowing for his unscheduled digression it should only have been a quarter to three. He looked at his watch for the first time, saw that it was nearly three thirty. That music was still playing inside his head; there was no way he could stop it. An icy tingle ran up and down his spine. Somehow three-quarters of an hour had passed, disappeared without trace. This was madness. He had only paused for two or three minutes to listen to the busker and the detour back to the car park would not have used up more than five minutes at the most.

'Where on earth have you been?' Brenda appeared in the doorway, an expression of anxiety on her pert features.

'I was longer at the bank than I thought.' He averted his gaze. She had an uncanny knack of detecting even the most innocuous lie.

'There's no problem, is there?'

'No,' he smiled, 'twenty grand if we need it. We spent most of the time just chatting.'

'Oh, I see.' She made no attempt to disguise her relief. 'But I think you'd better nip and fetch Ben. We can't impose on the Pocklingtons too much. However well Ben and Will get on together, there is a limit, and they've been good enough to have him down there a lot lately whilst we've been getting this place set up.'

'I'd better go right away.' He turned back towards the Land Rover. 'There's some patching up needed on that fence the goats have pulled down, but I guess another half hour won't make any difference. Unless, of course, they get through on to Pocklington's land. That'll be the end of our friendship, if you can call it that, with the Pocklingtons.'

'You'd better get a move on.' Brenda was agitated now. 'We don't want any bother.'

Dick wished that the neighbouring land had been owned by somebody other than Don and Avis Pocklington. Avis was fine: never had much to say but was always willing to help out if you needed it. He could not understand why she had married a man like Don, whose weasel-like features gave away his temperament. Small and wiry, he was one who worked from dawn until dusk but was never slow to unleash his quick temper if anything was not to his liking. His livestock, his family, and his neighbours were all likely to be on the receiving end of a tirade of abuse if they offended him in the slightest manner. He had been one of Dick's critics in the beginning, always ready with a jibe about 'playing at farming' and 'organic rubbish'. Dick had ignored the remarks and so far they had never clashed. You had to hand it to Don, he had begun with a fifty acre holding and now he was the biggest and wealthiest farmer in the district and he wasn't slow to let you know it. He had bought up one small farm after another, sold off the farmhouses to 'outsiders' requiring a country residence, kept the land and farmed it intensively. The environment had suffered in many ways as a result but Don's bank balance had swelled. He was disliked by the villagers and other farmers, renowned for his meanness. Dick prayed that the goats would not get through that gap in the fence until he had had a chance to repair it.

'How's it gone, Ben?'

Ben was playing on his own in the yard when Dick arrived. There was no sign of the Pocklingtons, not even young Will. They were so busy working, they had left a nine-year-old to amuse himself in a farmyard cluttered with potentially dangerous implements.

'OK,' Ben smiled but it failed to hide the loneliness in his expression. 'Mr Pocklington said at dinner time that they'd better start combining and Will had to help him. I could've gone with them but I didn't want to. He shouted at Mrs Pocklington because she was late with the dinner and it made Will cry. I don't want to come here again, Dad.'

'OK, we'll try not to send you. Maybe Will can come over and play with you instead.'

'They've just bought a new combine harvester,' Ben went on. 'Mr Pocklington says it cost him fifty grand. It's the latest kind, one of the first in this country. Will we ever be able to buy one, Dad?'

'I doubt it,' Dick smiled, 'and even if we made that sort of money I wouldn't spend it on modern machinery. Our corn will be stooked and threshed. That's what people pay to come to see.'

'I know.' Ben looked wistful. 'I told Will about how we'll be making a Corn Goat and he laughed, just like his dad. He said that was fine because at least it wouldn't get through gaps in fences and on to their land.'

A sly dig. Dick's lips tightened. Don Pocklington had obviously spotted those breaks in the fence and was eagerly anticipating a row with his neighbour. The man was despicable.

'I think maybe you'd better not go there again, after all.' He patted Ben's knee and wished again that that melody would stop plaguing him. Now he had a headache coming on.

The fencing repair was not as easy as Dick had anticipated. The goats had released the tension by standing with their forefeet on the wire to reach Pocklington's hawthorn hedge on the other side, so instead of a straightforward patching-up job with a piece of cut-off netting, the tension needed to be rectified with a wire-strainer. Fortunately there was such a tool in the back of the Land Rover.

The netting had buckled under the animals' weight, pulled the staples out of the fence post. It was almost an hour before Dick was satisfied with the repair job. And, throughout, that annoying music echoed in his brain. He found himself trying to compose lyrics to suit it. He attempted to hum a country and western tune in an effort to rid his memory of the other but it didn't work. And his headache still lingered on.

Finished at last. He tossed the tools into the rear of the vehicle, paused to wipe the sweat from his forehead with his arm. It was only then that he became aware that something was wrong. There was no sign of the goats! Usually at the first hint of a human presence their acute hearing had them running to investigate, hindering you with their natural inquisitiveness. Once Abby, the more mischievous of the pair, had picked up a bag of nails and the contents had spilled out into the long grass. He had spent almost a quarter of an hour picking them up. Maybe they were below the brow of the hill. Just as long as they had not strayed through the gap on to Pocklington's farm. . .

Dick walked to the brow of the meadow slope, peered over. The grass had browned during the long heatwave; maybe they had found lush grazing down below where the wood shaded the pastureland. He peered into the bright sunlight; it stabbed into his eyes, worsened his headache. He squinted, picked out a white shape standing on its hindlegs in order to reach an elderberry branch. That was Abby all right. He scanned the boundary hedge right up to the apex and down the other side. There was no sign of Gubbins.

'Shuddup!' He yelled aloud at the music inside his head which had suddenly stepped up a few decibels. Blast it, Gubbins must have got through on to the neighbouring field. He should not have lingered to listen to that damned busker. Half an hour earlier and he might have repaired the break in time. He'd better get over into the adjoining field, pray that Don Pocklington was too busy combining his wheat to notice, and get that stubborn goat back. If. . .

That was when he heard Ben screaming up in the barley field.

Dick broke into a run, forgot his headache, forgot Gubbins. The only thing he could not ignore was that weird melody which seemed to mock him from within, speeding, slowing, speeding up again. It hammered inside his skull, vibrated his whole body, tortured him with every uphill step.

God, what had happened to Ben? He could hear him screaming above the imaginary harmonica, screeching hysterically. Maybe he had been bitten by an adder. Or he had ripped himself clambering over some barbed wire. Or. . .

Ben was running towards him, fleeing blindly from some unknown terror, his screams now reduced to sobs. He did not appear to be injured, or he could not have run like that. There was no sign of any blood. Nobody else was in sight.

'Ben!'

The boy neither heard nor saw his father. His features were deathly white, his eyes were closed. Then he was bowling over, stubbing his foot against a tussock, sprawling on the perched grass.

'*No!*' The boy managed a final scream, struggled and fought, eyes tightly closed.

'Ben, it's me. Daddy!'

Ben's writhings ceased. He went limp, and for a moment Dick thought that his son had fainted. Then an eye flickered partly open and the boy peered fearfully from beneath a half-closed lid, shuddering violently, afraid of what he might see.

'Daddy!' It was always 'Daddy' when Ben was upset. Deathly white, he clung to his father, tiny fingers pinching in his anguish, burying his face against Dick's shirt. 'Daddy, don't let him get me. *Please!*'

'Who, Ben?' Dick's eyes roved the landscape but there was nobody in sight. If Ben was fleeing from some child molester, some pervert, then Dick would take the law into his own hands. 'There's nobody here, Ben. Are you sure you're not imagining things? You're safe now. Just tell me what it was that scared you.'

'A little. . . man!' The child gulped, could scarcely get the words out, and when he did the tremor made them almost inaudible.

'Look, Ben.' Dick lifted up his son, cradled him in his arms the way he used to do when Ben was a toddler only just learning to walk. 'There's nobody around, I promise. I think the best thing we can do is go back home and then you can tell me and Mummy all about it.'

Ben started to cry, sobbing uncontrollably. And it was only when Dick reached the Land Rover that he was suddenly aware that that dreadful melody inside his head had stopped. And his headache was gone with it.

'What on earth's happened?' Brenda wrung her hands together, went suddenly pallid as her husband walked into the kitchen carrying Ben in his arms. 'Oh, my God!'

'Take it easy,' Dick laid their son on the couch, knelt by his side. 'He's OK, just had some kind of fright. Tell us what frightened you, Ben.'

'A. . . little. . . man.'

Dick sighed, looked away. This was ridiculous, but they had to humour the boy. Quite obviously something had terrified him, real or imaginary, and they had to know what it was before they could allay his fears.

'What kind of little man, Ben?' Brenda spoke softly, squeezed his hand to reassure him. 'Come on, you can tell us, and if he's still around Daddy will soon give him what for.'

'A. . .' Ben hesitated, his eyes roaming the room as if he expected to see the object of his terror lurking in some shadowy corner. 'A little. . . *corn man!*'

'A corn man! You mean a corn dolly?'

'Yes, yes.'

'Well corn dollies can't hurt you, they're only made of corn. They can't move. Or talk. Or do anything.'

'This one did!' The boy's eyes rolled, he checked the room again. *'He came out of the barley, made horrible shrieking noises and started to run after me. If he'd caught me, he'd've killed me!'*

'Nonsense!' Dick said.

'It's not nonsense!' Ben was becoming petulant the way he often did when something had frightened him. 'He was real and alive and he meant to kill me. *I swear on the Holy Bible I'm not lying!*' His voice rose to a shrill pitch which bordered on that earlier screaming.

'All right, all right, we believe you.' Dick glanced at Brenda, saw fear in her eyes, too. Not because she believed in evil little corn men who chased young children but because their son was more terrified than ever they had known him before.

'How about going up to bed?' Brenda stooped as though to lift him up. 'You're exhausted, and when you wake up in the morning you'll feel better and it won't seem half as bad. Then we'll all talk about it at breakfast and. . .'

'No! Don't leave me alone in my bedroom. Let me sleep with you tonight. Please!'

'All right.' This was one issue that Brenda was not going to contest. Whatever Ben might or might not have seen, there was no mistaking his terror. More than likely he would have nightmares. 'You can sleep in with us tonight, Ben. But it's a long way off bedtime yet, so how about if you just lie there for a while, eh? I've got some baking to do and you can watch me.'

'All right,' the boy nodded. His initial fear seemed to have subsided. 'But I promise it was a corn man and he was alive.'

'I'll go and take a look.' Dick reached into the cupboard, took out his shotgun, an ancient double-barrelled hammer gun. 'And if I see him, Ben, I'll give him both barrels. And I'll bring him back to show you and Mummy can put him on the woodstove!'

All three of them laughed but it sounded forced.

Instead of taking the Land Rover Dick walked up to the barley field. The gun was cradled in the crook of his arm, cartridges in the breech. Not that he believed in live corn dollies for one moment but in his terror Ben might have seen a stoat or a weasel, and those fierce little predators were capable of causing carnage in any poultry shed where they managed to gain entrance. Dick's thoughts turned to his bronze turkeys, the ducks and geese which they had reared for the Christmas market. If a rabbit showed up then he would shoot it, bring it home for the pot and try to convince his son that it was all a case of mistaken identity. And at the same time Dick would go on up to the knoll which commanded a view of the surrounding farmland to see if he could spot the missing Gubbins.

The sun was beginning to dip in the western sky, a huge ball of fire which promised yet another day of scorching late summer sunshine on the morrow. There was no prospect of any rain yet. The drought might last for weeks. Next week they would begin the corn harvest; the barley was ready. In the distance he heard the steady drone of a combine harvester. Don Pocklington would work by headlights until the dew halted him. He did not trust weather forecasts any more than he trusted his neighbours. He was that kind of man. Dick headed up to the knoll. He was uneasy about his missing goat.

He stood there at the summit of the straw-like grassy hillock and surveyed the fields in every direction. In the far distance he could just make out the trundling, growling yellow monster that was Pocklington's combine harvester. Fields of sugar beet and swedes, another expanse of grain where once there had been six or seven smaller fields until Don had grubbed out the hedgerows and created a barley plain; the village beyond the railway line and further still the unsightly cooling towers of the power station.

In the opposite direction lay the city, the spires of the cathedral golden in the rays of the dying sun. He searched the foreground carefully, checked every tree and bush that might have hidden a stubborn goat which had discovered lusher pastures beyond her own boundaries. But there was no sign of Gubbins and Dick Kirby's stomach muscles knotted until he felt slightly sick.

Dusk was deepening by the time he reached his own five acre cornfield, ripe barley that bowed its multitude of heads in readiness for the binder. A soft breeze rippled through it, rustled it. Dick rested his gun up against the gate post, felt for his pipe and tobacco pouch. On any other day except today he could have relaxed, waited here for darkness to fall, savoured the tranquillity. Except that Gubbins was missing and Ben was nearly out of his mind with fright.

The boy was not usually fanciful. Certainly something had scared him, there was no getting away from that. But it had to be something quite ordinary. Like a stoat or a weasel, maybe even a rabbit half glimpsed in the corn, squealing its terror when one of those fierce predators bore it to the ground and began to suck its blood from a vicious jugular wound.

Suddenly Dick tensed, forgot his pipe and found himself instinctively reaching for his gun. Something was definitely moving out there in the corn, brushing a path to and fro; stopping, starting again. Carefully, soundlessly, he eased the hammers back, cocked the gun. Damnation, it was too dark to see clearly now even if whatever it was showed itself. He thought about firing a couple of barrels into the barley, told himself not to be so bloody stupid. One never shot at an unidentified quarry. Likewise, even if it was a stoat or weasel, the chances of hitting it were minimal. He waited, shotgun raised in readiness.

Then it screeched, high-pitched and piercing, a scream that was neither animal nor human, prickling the nape of his neck. His mouth was dry, his legs went suddenly weak, and the gun in his hands seemed puny protection against a being that could scream its malevolence with such ferocity and evil.

Dick backed away, treading as stealthily as he could, all the time still trying to convince himself that it was nothing more than a predatory mammal, that his nerves were stretched to the point where, like Ben, he would believe almost anything.

Once clear of the barley field, he began to walk quickly, his trembling legs hastening him homewards. For some inexplicable reason his train of tortured thought led back to the busker in the square. And that was when the unrelenting music inside his head started up again.

As he approached the farmhouse another sound penetrated the lilting, eerie melody, seemed to keep time with it crazily. It was some moments before he recognized it, knew without any doubt that what he heard was the plaintive bleating of a goat. Not Abby; when you kept goats you came to identify their voices. The one that was calling to him now on the vibrating echoes of that busker's harmonica was, without any doubt, Gubbins.

And, wherever she was, she was pleading with him to help her.

CHAPTER THREE

It was almost midday when Dick started the corn harvest. In the distance he could hear the steady progressive drone of Don Pocklington's combine harvester. The other had started shortly after nine, was desperate to finish his entire crop of grain before the end of the week.

But for Dick it was more than just harvesting a field of barley. This was his first showpiece, a demonstration of how corn was gathered in bygone years. Up on the brow of the hill was a small post and rail enclosure where, hopefully, an audience would watch from. The *Mercury* would give him some useful coverage; a reporter and photographer were scheduled to arrive in the early afternoon. He hoped by then a few members of the public would have arrived and paid their £2 for a tour of the farm. Brenda would take them round.

Dick planned to spread his small harvest over two days; the weather would stay fine at least until the weekend. He would cut one half of the field today, the remainder tomorrow, stack the corn in stooks, and then carry them back to the yard for threshing on Sunday. With luck there would be a small influx of visitors and that was when Brenda would fashion the traditional Corn Goat, a crude effigy of a goat made from the straw, pandering to an age-old superstition. Not that Dick or Brenda were superstitious, but they were trying to re-create tradition. Dick was meticulous where detail was concerned; he had to get it right in every aspect.

He had considered the possibility of hiring shire horses to pull the grass-mower. At least three animals would be necessary to tow the heavy implement up and down the field. Maybe next time if everything went well. For the moment his old 1954 David Brown tractor with its upright exhaust that belched black fumes would suffice. That was traditional enough for the moment.

He was worried about Ben. Something had scared him to hell two nights ago, and after Dick had heard that. shrill, piping screaming in the corn he knew how the boy felt. Dick had heard the cry of a rabbit brought down by a stoat or a weasel before. . . but it hadn't sounded *quite* like that. *The screeching in the barley had sounded almost. . . human!*

He told himself it was nonsense, his nerves were getting the better of him, strained by the niggling possibility of a twenty grand overdraft to finance a project that might not take off. In spite of the so-called 'green revolution', when members of the public were heavily into energy saving and environmentally friendly products, would they really put their money where theirs mouths were? Would they pay two quid for the privilege of witnessing chemical-free farming using methods retrieved from the days of their forefathers? Was it just a passing phase before everybody took the easy way out and returned to a lethargic as-before lifestyle? Only time would tell. Maybe he should have hired those horses after all. Even if diesel fumes caused less pollution than petrol, villainous clouds pumping out of the exhaust were hardly an advertisement for that which he was preaching.

He began a slow tour of the field's perimeter, cutting a wide swathe that would enable him to line the machinery up for mowing crosswise. The land dipped steeply in places, gave him a sense of vertigo. If the brakes failed then he would career out of control down the slope, crash through the flimsy fence and straggling hedge, go right on down until he overturned at the bottom of Pocklington's meadow by the river. They wouldn't fail; he had checked the tractor over only last week. He was just edgy. Like Ben.

The grain yield would be low this year after the dry summer and Dick was grateful that his main income would come from tourism. Hopefully. He glanced behind him, caught a final glimpse of the spectators' enclosure before the tractor dipped below the skyline. There were four or five people up there, probably a family. Even the sparsest audience was encouraging on your first day.

There was still no sign of Gubbins and that was worrying. She had to be somewhere on Pocklington's extensive farmland, in all probability wandering on and on, browsing as she went, the grazing ahead always more appealing than the one she was in. She would need milking or problems would arise. Mastitis would set in. Yesterday Brenda had phoned Avis, choosing a time when she knew Don would be combining. No, they hadn't seen a stray goat, but they'd phone if they did. Right now they were too busy with the corn harvest. Don would phone all right if he spotted Gubbins, a tirade of abuse and obscenities. Dick flinched at the thought, but rather that than lose a goat.

Dick reached the bottom of the sloping field, turned sharply to follow the boundary hedge. It seemed strange having to take your time. Last year he had cut the entire field in one day, carried it the next. And they hadn't had to bother with a Corn Goat. Now it was a different venture, a whole new ball game.

It was on the uphill slope that a movement in the barley attracted his attention, a rippling that had the ears parting, swaying. Dick tensed, slowed momentarily, felt his pulses start to race. It wasn't the wind because the atmosphere was still. Something was moving in there, running to escape the oncoming tractor and mower.

Suddenly, a pearly grey body burst up out of the grain, a bird the size of a pheasant that screeched an angry *get-back-get-back* cry of alarm, flying low and fast, then dropping back down in the centre of the field.

He laughed aloud with sheer relief, saw how his hands on the steering wheel trembled. It was only a gallini, one of his flock of twenty that spent most of their time scratching round the farmyard, perching on the gate and screeching deafeningly at the approach of a stranger, sometimes even at himself. Of course, the birds were attracted by the ripe corn, a day's gleaning to fill their crops. In all probability the rest of them were in the barley, too. That was fine, as long as they didn't stray across to Pocklington's cornfields. Which they surely would eventually, but by then there would only be acres of stubble remaining. All the same, Don would complain even though the birds were not doing any harm.

Another thought crossed Dick's mind and this time his relief was almost overwhelming. That screeching cry from the barley the other night, it was probably one of the guineafowl. The sound wasn't quite right but these birds made peculiar noises at times. Didn't they? On the other hand, they surely wouldn't be out in the fields at deep dusk, they would be roosting in the thorn bushes behind the house. Just an odd gallini, maybe, a greedy cock bird that was determined to stuff its crop to bursting point before retiring for the night. Somehow Dick convinced himself, because it was the easy way out, a means of putting his mind at rest when there was no other feasible explanation. He would try to convince Ben, too, that what he had seen in the grain was nothing more malevolent that a cock gallini angry at being disturbed during its feeding.

Brenda was worried about a number of things. Nagging fears that were in no way related and yet combined into an overwhelming feeling of depression. She wasn't happy about her husband's meeting with the bank manager; £20,000 overdrafts might have an initial euphoria about them when you were embarking upon a new enterprise but at the end of the day they had to be repaid. With hard earned cash. And the interest was too frightening to contemplate.

Something had happened to Gubbins for sure. The obvious explanation for the goat's disappearance was that she had strayed on to the neighbouring farmland. Even so, the animal ought to have found her way back before nightfall. She always returned to the yard, bleating impatiently for her bucket of concentrates, demanding to be milked. She might have been stolen. Brenda wondered if there were any gypsies or hippies camped out in the vicinity. If it wasn't for the possibility that a number of visitors might turn up to watch the harvest, she would have gone to look for the missing animal.

Ben was her greatest concern. The boy was obviously very frightened, distressed by that which he claimed to have seen the day before yesterday. She had given up trying to explain to him that corn dollies were inanimate objects that were hung up at harvest time, remnants of ancient superstition. He would not accept that it might have been a stoat or a weasel he saw, even a rabbit. He was adamant that it was a little corn man, chasing him angrily.

Their son had slept in their bed on the night after his trauma. Once he had woken up, screaming in the aftermath of some nightmare. The next night both she and Dick had insisted that Ben slept in his own room; this couldn't go on night after night. Sometime in the early hours she had woken up, some sixth sense warning her that somebody was moving about on the landing. It was Ben, sleepwalking. He might have fallen down the narrow staircase, broken a limb. Without waking him, she had led him gently back to his room. He was still there, sleeping in late. Doubtless, he needed to catch up on his rest after two nights of troubled slumber.

Brenda was in a dilemma. Already a family had arrived in the yard, eager to witness old-time farming methods. She had taken their money, suggested that they walked up the rough track to where there was a viewpoint from which they could watch the start of the corn harvest. She ought to have accompanied them, delivered a lecture on traditional methods and organic farming. But she dared not leave Ben. Maybe he would wake up soon and then she could send him on up to the tourists. He would relish the role of guide and it would take his mind off his fears.

That same uncanny sense which had warned her of Ben's nocturnal ramblings began to trouble her again, even stronger this time. There was somebody outside in the yard. She had not heard a vehicle, so maybe it was the visitors returning. Dissatisfied, disillusioned customers, come to demand their money back because this was all a big con, there was nothing to warrant paying two quid for. She could not hear anybody outside but she knew they were there, felt a presence as if whoever was there was calling to her to come outside. Her mouth went suddenly dry, and she found herself wishing that Dick was here.

She glanced back towards the stairs, listened intently. There was no movement from above. Ben still slept. She ought not to leave him. You're not going to leave him, you're only going to the door to see who's out there. I don't want to see. You have to. The calling was stronger now. Hurry.

She almost ran to the door, scraped it open across the uneven quarry tiles. She blinked in the bright sunlight, and then caught her breath in dismay at the figure which confronted her. She wanted to slam the door shut again but for some reason her body refused to obey her instincts.

The stranger was obviously a hippy, she concluded; those soiled and greasy denims would have long been discarded by anybody else, even a labourer. The straggling beard, those piercing dark eyes, frightened her so that she recoiled mentally. Dangling from a frayed cord around his neck was a battered old mouth organ that glinted as it reflected the sunlight, dazzling her.

Her lips moved but no words came from them and, anyway, she had no idea what she was trying to say. She felt herself trembling violently, her legs seeming scarcely able to support the weight of her body. She leaned against the creaking door, otherwise she might have fallen.

'Good morning.' His voice was cultured, softly spoken. 'I'm sorry if I've disturbed you, but is this the traditional working farm?'

'Yes.' Her voice sounded far away, a whisper.

'I'd like to look round,' he held out a hand that was clean and white in contrast to his appearance, with no ingrained dirt or callouses, the nails manicured, two pound coins nestling in the palm. 'I'll find my own way round if that's all right with you.'

'That's fine.' She tried to think of an excuse, a plausible reason that would have sent him back whence he had come. But there was none. If you embarked upon an enterprise such as this one, then you attracted idealists, folks from all walks of life. You were bound to get a few eccentrics, you had to accept them. Besides, she was still worrying about that overdraft. They could not afford to refuse paying customers.

'Thank you.' He smiled, revealing a set of even, shining white teeth. 'I must compliment you upon the good work you are doing, preaching the recipe for survival. Man is hell-bent upon a course for disaster, poisoning the land and polluting the atmosphere. Unless something is done soon, this planet will become an arid wasteland, interspersed with radioactive oceans in which nothing is able to live. Perhaps it is already too late.'

Brenda was aware how she trembled, not because this stranger was frightening but rather because his words carried a chilling sincerity. For some inexplicable reason she found herself attracted to him. His charisma was irresistible; he was the kind of man you could turn to in a crisis. And she had known him less than a couple of minutes.

'We've lost a goat.' Instinctively she found herself confiding her troubles in him. 'A milking nanny. She just went off and hasn't come back.' Somehow she prevented herself from telling him about Ben's fear of corn dollies who chased after young children. She had not intended to tell him about Gubbins, the words had just slipped out. Something cold

34

chilled her sweaty palm; she had no recollection of accepting this man's admission fee but the two pound coins glinted up at her.

'I shouldn't worry.' Another reassuring smile. He had stepped back a pace. 'She will be back, I have no doubt. Sometimes animals just. . . go somewhere and then return.'

Brenda felt dizzy. A wave of faintness had her holding on to the door again. 'Who are you?' She had not intended to ask him outright, but her curiosity had got out of control. Mutely she was already apologising, it was none of her business; this was a free country, folks came and went as they pleased.

'My name's Jonjo.' He met her gaze until she flinched, averted her eyes. 'A lot of people know me. Most farmers allow me to spend a night in their outbuildings.'

'You're welcome.' She almost curtseyed, knew that she was blushing. She also experienced a pang of guilt because she knew that Dick would never allow a ragbag wanderer to remain on the farm overnight.

'Thank you.' He gave a short bow. 'If the necessity arises, then I shall accept your hospitality with gratitude. In the meantime, I am eager to view the age-old methods of husbandry.'

He turned on his heel and she watched him walk away, proud and agile, heading towards the track which led up to the barley field. In the distance she could hear the hum of the old David Brown.

'Mum!' A shout from the top of the stairs jerked her back to reality. Ben was up and about, checking on her whereabouts. She knew by his tone that he needed to know she was there because, even in the daylight, his fear persisted.

'I'm here, darling.'

'Mum, who was that man?' Ben moved down the staircase, stopped halfway, an expression of amazement on his pallid features.

'What man?' She did not know why she was stalling, only that her son might imagine fresh terrors in the sight of a filth-clad traveller.

'The one you were talking to, the one with the beard and the mouth organ. His voice woke me up. I was watching from the bedroom window.'

'He told me his name was Jonjo.' She shivered in spite of the heat of the day. 'Just a tramp. But he's paid two pounds to look round.'

'Can I go and show him round, Mum?'

'*No!*' Her refusal bordered on a shriek, an emphatic denial. 'You're not to talk to strangers. How many times have you to be told?'

'Aw, Mum.' Ben was crestfallen. 'Jonjo's all right, you know he is. I like the look of him and he's got a nice voice.'

'He's a tramp!' Another sensation of guilt flooded over her. 'Your father would be angry with you if you got talking to him.' But not me because I think the guy's OK, too. 'You can stop with me for a while and then we'll both go up to the cornfield. And if Jonjo's still there we'll both see him again.'

Strangely, frighteningly, the idea was appealing to her.

Dick had cut approximately half of the barley crop by mid-afternoon. He sat with the tractor engine idling, glanced up towards the visitors' vantage point where a small crowd of maybe fifteen or twenty people had gathered. That was encouraging. He had feared nobody might turn up.

He shaded his eyes against the glare of the sun, waited whilst the distant silhouettes became vaguely recognizable. He picked out Brenda and, thankfully, Ben standing alongside her; it was gratifying to see that the family which had arrived first had stayed throughout. And. . . he squinted, could not really be certain from this distance, but that figure on the end, wearing a jacket in spite of the heat, a hat pushed back on his head. . . It took a moment or two for recognition to register with a shock that had him stiffening in his seat. He might be mistaken, he hoped that he was. . . The fellow turned, began to walk away, back straight, a kind of march that might have been comical anywhere but here.

The busker from the market square!

Dick stared after the other until he was lost over the skyline, felt the sweat on his body beginning to chill. That guy was up to no good. He didn't want him mooching around the farm. Hippies stole things, littered the environment with their rubbish, smoked pot and had a host of other undesirable, obnoxious habits. He was angry with Brenda for admitting the fellow. He tensed, and then that weird melody started up inside his head, had him clasping his ears in a futile attempt to stifle it.

'Well, I think we can be well satisfied with our first "open" day.' Brenda prepared a salad supper on the working surface in the kitchen, deliberately kept her back towards her husband. She sensed Dick was displeased with her, hoped that the matter would not be voiced. Ben was seated at the table next to his father, eyes half closed. He might fall asleep before the meal was served.

'Thirty-seven.' Dick's tone was clipped. 'Twenty-four adults and thirteen children. A total of fifty-five pounds fifty pence gate money. Not bad, and maybe we can improve on that tomorrow and at the weekend after our advert appears in the *Mercury*. By the way, don't let any more hippies in. We don't want them sussing the place out. The next we'll know is that they've been back and pinched the chainsaw and anything else they can find. Gubbins is already missing.'

'Jonjo wouldn't steal anything!" Ben's eyes flickered open, his voice was suddenly defiant.

'Who?'

'Jonjo, the man with the beard and the mouth organ. He's all right, and Mum says he told her that Gubbins will come back before long.'

'Which means the damned fellow knows where she is!' Dick's fist thumped the table, rattled the cutlery. 'And you two have even got on first name terms with him! Look, I don't want that fellow hanging around here. If I catch him again, I'll throw him out myself!'

Brenda dropped the salad servers, jumped as they clattered on the floor. 'He probably won't be back, anyway,' she muttered without looking round. 'He hasn't done any harm and at least he paid to come in. In fact, he seemed quite educated.'

'Most of them are.' Her husband was scathing. 'University students who have opted for a lazy, unwashed way of life whilst the taxpayer foots the bill. Just let me catch him around the place!'

'I bet he'd know how to deal with corn men.' Ben's voice was shrill, angry. 'Jonjo wouldn't be scared of them.'

'As for your so-called corn men,' Dick Kirby rounded on his son, rapped on the tabletop, 'I realized today what they are. The damned gallinis have found their way up to the barley. That's what you saw, Ben.'

Ben stared at his father, shook his head slowly. 'It wasn't a gallini, Dad. I know what gallinis look like. This was a little corn man, and if he'd caught me he would've killed me. I know he would.'

Dick was exhausted but sleep eluded him. His head ached from the hot sun but at least that music in his head had stopped. The night was stifling. He was tempted to throw the single sheet off the bed but undoubtedly Brenda would wake up and complain that she was cold. So he lay there, staring up into the darkened room, his thoughts flitting from Gubbins to Ben. And always they returned to the man who called himself Jonjo.

In all probability they would not see the busker again; it had been a chance call by an environmentally obsessed idealist. Dick was willing to bet the fellow was an animal liberation activist and a vegetarian to boot. Which presented a threat to the penned poultry. He might return one night and let out all the birds, and as a result the foxes would have a field day. And Dick was certain – he had almost convinced himself that he was – that Ben's corn dolly was nothing more than a gallini, the one which he himself had heard in the corn a couple of nights ago. Gubbins was somewhere on Pocklington's land, and after the corn harvest was finished he would go and search for her. After he'd found her everything would be fine.

Sleep was slipping even further from his grasp. Tomorrow he would finish cutting the barley, bind it into stooks. Another press photographer was scheduled to come up and take some pictures of Brenda making the Corn Goat. After that they would bring the harvest home in style on the trailer behind the David Brown. A couple of sheaves and the crudely fashioned straw goat had been promised to the village church for the harvest festival. The Reverend Elmhurst had requested that some more sheaves be sent up to the cathedral. Traditional farming techniques were suddenly in demand. It was excellent publicity.

Dick found himself wondering about the busker again. His thoughts returned to that gathering in the square, the way children and teenagers had been drawn by the music. There was something eerie about the notes, like an ancient tune that some wandering minstrel might have played in order to ward off evil spirits centuries ago. Or to call them up. Dick shivered in spite of the balmy night atmosphere, and that was when he heard that haunting melody again. He tossed restlessly, decided that it might have been a proliferation of 'Greensleeves'. There was no way he was going to rid himself of it.

Strangely, this time it had the effect of making him drowsy, its compulsion that of a lullaby. His eyelids drooped. It sounded so far away, as though the busker was playing back in the city and the night wind had borne the sound to him across fields and meadows. Dick's senses began to drift and only when he was sliding gently down into slumber's deep abyss did the realization strike him that the music was not just lingering echoes in his brain. It was coming from somewhere outside, maybe even as close as the paddock adjoining the farmyard.

CHAPTER FOUR

Brenda Kirby felt slightly sick and the hand which nervously brushed back her fair hair trembled. She experienced an urge to flee, a panic that fluttered in her taut stomach. With a conscious effort she threw it off, took a deep breath and let it out slowly. In a moment of nostalgic terror, she recalled this very same feeling the night she had gone on stage at the village hall to play Dorothy in a junior school presentation of *The Wizard of Oz*.

Nothing much had changed. A real cornfield instead of stage scenery, a flowery dress that she herself had made, in a style that would have been widely worn at the beginning of the century. And an audience which pressed forward eagerly, all eyes focused on her.

She smiled, hoped that nobody noticed how her lower lip quivered and the hands that gathered up corn straw trembled. She had never made a Corn Goat before. With hindsight and time to spare she would have made a trial run last night, but the harvest and recent events had relegated this traditional ceremony to a triviality. Suddenly it was of major importance. The sixty or so spectators were anticipating an exhibition of age-old craftsmanship. She must not disappoint them. She prayed that she wouldn't make a fool of herself and tried to recall how that woman at the Royal Show had fashioned her goat. It had looked simplicity itself then.

Brenda smiled, allowed her gaze to travel in a half circle. The visitors had been allowed to move down from their vantage point up on the skyline, were gathered around the tractor and trailer loaded with the last of the sheaves. Dick sat on the tractor, Ben on his knee. She scrutinized the sea of faces, relaxed because there was no bearded harmonica player amongst them. Jonjo would have detected her anxiety, recognized her for the fraud she was. Only Dick and Ben knew, smiled their encouragement. These people haven't a clue, anyway, so bluff them. Make *something*.

She took her time, pulled straws, began to plait them. Heads craned forward. Maybe she was expected to provide a detailed commentary? At least words would help to cover up her incompetence.

'Up to a century or so ago, farmers always made an effigy of a goat from the straw to accompany the last trailerload of sheaves.' Empty words off the top of her head, talking for talking's sake. 'An ancient custom that dates back centuries. This goat,' well, at least it was taking on a vague animal shape, 'is an embodiment of the corn spirit and it will live in the granary throughout the winter months, protect the grain from mould and vermin.' Actually Tibs, the black and white cat, would keep the mice and rats down. She wasn't sure about the mould. If the barley was dry enough then it should be all right. 'According to custom, we must send a sheaf to a neighbouring farmer who has not yet finished his harvest. For luck.' Certainly Don Pocklington would not appreciate the gesture!

The shape was forming: a head and a body, four legs twisting out of the bundle. Now for the horns. . . Her anxiety merged into relief. It wasn't bad for a first attempt. She knelt, set it up on the stubble; it stood firmly, roughly the size of a terrier. Somebody in the audience started to clap, others took up this show of appreciation. If they were just being kind then their gesture was very welcome. Brenda was sweating. Her bluff had worked.

Her thoughts switched to Gubbins. They would have to find her soon. If only Jonjo would show up again then she would ask him what he had meant, plead with him if necessary to evoke the return of their favourite milking goat. Dick claimed that the busker had been somewhere around the farm last night, that he had heard him playing. He had been angry about it, threatened to phone the police. Maybe it was better if Jonjo didn't return, after all.

The gallinis were calling further down the stubble field, out of sight below the brow, screeching in a deafening crescendo. They were angry because the grain had been harvested, that only the gleanings remained for them. They were ill tempered, quarrelsome birds. Brenda wished that Dick would reduce the flock. Before long their equally bad-tempered neighbour was sure to lodge a complaint, even if they only strayed on to his pastureland.

Dick started up the tractor, belched a cloud of diesel fumes into the atmosphere. Brenda turned, placed the Corn Goat amidst the sheaves, and climbed up on to the back. Another hurdle was out of the way. Tomorrow they would concentrate on the threshing. She gave a sigh of relief. At least the public were showing an interest.

'It really is a superb Corn Goat, Mrs Kirby.' The Reverend Elmhurst's rotund features beamed his admiration of the effigy as he held it carefully, adjusted the straw legs so that it stood on the scrubbed pine table. 'Absolutely superb! I'm sure that it will be the focal point of the harvest festival decorations.'

'Thank you.' Brenda blushed her embarrassment. The vicar had a knack of making her feel guilty, probably because she never attended Sunday services and yet he went out of his way to be friendly towards her. Bald head glinting in the artificial light, he was the classic country clergyman, rotund and fresh-faced, always dressed in a tweed jacket with leather elbow patches and baggy grey flannel trousers that were shiny around the seat. On Friday evenings he was usually to be found in the bar of the Dog Inn, his way of demonstrating to his parishioners that he was one of them, that alcohol in moderation was no sin.

'Oh, and I wonder if I could ask a favour on behalf of the dean and chapter.' His slight nervousness might have been affected. 'I wonder if you would be good enough to deliver the sheaves tomorrow, Mr Kirby. The cathedral is to be decorated in preparation for the harvest festival a day or two earlier than previously scheduled. Would you mind?'

'No, of course not,' Dick replied, groaned inwardly because tomorrow they would have a paying audience for the threshing display. Doubtless, he would fit the trip up to the Close in somehow.

'The earlier the better.' Elmhurst drained his tea cup. 'Thank you so much. And whatever's the matter with you, young man?' His smile changed to a frown as his eyes narrowed and focused on Ben, who sat staring at the Corn Goat, visibly trembling.

Ben's lips moved, his Adam's apple bobbled, but no sound came from his mouth. His features were deathly white, and his eyes protruded like water bubbles stretching until they must surely burst.

'Ben.' Brenda thought her son was on the verge of a fit. She moved towards him but Dick beat her to it.

'Benjie, snap out of it!' He hoped it sounded firm but kindly but there was no disguising the note of panic in his tone. His fingers closed over the boy's shoulder, shook him gently. 'Ben!'

'Oh, my goodness!' The Reverend Elmhurst's complexion had paled. His hand jerked, knocked again at the straw effigy, toppled it over so that it rattled crockery, spilled a half-full cup of tea.

And Ben screamed.

The shock seemed to loosen the words jammed in Ben's throat. They came out staccato, shook with terror. 'The goat. . . It's. . . it's. . .*Gubbins!*'

'Nonsense, darling.' Brenda pulled him close to her, cradled him to her bosom. 'It's only a heap of straw. *I* made it.'

'It's Gubbins!' The boy was adamant, defiant, sobbing now. 'Ask Jonjo, he'll tell you that's Gubbins.'

'He's over-tired, exhausted.' Dick spoke to the vicar, an angry apology. 'Ben had a fright the other night, a gallini chased him out of the corn. He thought it was. . . something else.'

'It was a little corn man,' Ben screeched, struggled in Brenda's grasp.

41

'He would've killed me if he'd caught me!'

'I'll have to go.' Elmhurst glanced at his watch, his wrist shaking. 'I must go and lock up the church. And thank you so much for. . . this, Mrs Kirby.' He seemed to be holding the straw goat at arm's length. 'I'll go and put it in the church right now.' Because I'm scared to sleep with it in the vicarage.

'Ben had better sleep in with us tonight,' Dick said, turning to Brenda after the door had closed behind the vicar. 'We can't have this nonsense going on night after night. And I'll tell you one thing,' he paused, shook a clenched fist, 'if I so much as hear a mouth organ tonight I'm going right out there, and God help that tramp if I get my hands on him!'

And that was when the music started up again inside Dick Kirby's throbbing skull.

When Dick stirred the next morning his first thought was that he had awakened early. Instead of the customary bright early morning sunshine slanting in through the chinks in the bedroom curtains, there was a depressing greyness that was reminiscent of the dawn. He padded across to the window, stared out at the blanket of grey vapour that enshrouded the farmyard, could barely discern the outline of the grain store opposite.

The first autumnal mist had arrived on the heels of the waning summer, determined to stamp its mark on the changing seasons even though the weather was stubbornly defying the calendar. A crow croaked from the branches of an oak tree, angry because it was unable to scavenge for its breakfast. The damp stillness was unexpected, eerie. The fog had crept in under cover of darkness, surprised man and beast. Later the sun's rays would disperse it but for the moment it refused to lift. If anything, it was thickening, Dick thought.

'What's the matter?' Brenda enquired sleepily, instinctively slipping an arm round Ben as though to satisfy herself that the corn creatures which he feared so vehemently had not spirited him away.

'Fog.' Dick turned and groped for his clothes on the chair. 'I guess it's about time, the weather's fooled us. From now on it's an Indian summer.'

'I'd better get up.' She withdrew her arm from Ben. He did not stir.

'No hurry.' Dick slid his feet into his slippers. 'I've got to go round the livestock first. We're not due to start threshing till midday, anyway, and with this mist we're unlikely to see any early customers.'

It was cold and clammy outside and he paused to fasten his jacket. That crow cawed again from the topmost bough of the mighty oak but it made no move to glide away. Which was strange, indeed. Dick stared up at it. Usually corvines fled at the approach of man. He shivered, but his goosepimples could not have been attributed solely to the damp rawness of the morning.

He opened the pop-hole of the turkey house. Every morning they spilled out fast, jostled one another in a race to be first at the corn trough in the wire run. This morning not one showed itself. He peered in through the aperture in the coop, saw how they all huddled at the far end of the perches. They were clearly frightened of something. Maybe a fox had been prowling outside during the night.

'Oh, well, please yourselves!' Dick kicked a stone angrily as he crossed the yard, spoke aloud as though he needed to hear a human voice, even his own.

It was the same everywhere; the Jacob's sheep were crowded into a corner of the pasture when they should have been grazing the dewy grass, even in the thickest fog. Abby was lying at the back of the goatshed, not interested in being milked. Perhaps she was pining for Gubbins.

And where the hell were the gallinis? He did not find them until he was on his way back into the house, a movement up on the misty roof attracting his attention. He stood there, stared in amazement, counted the hunched shapes on the gable end just to make sure. All twenty guineafowl were perched there, uncharacteristically silent, no harsh warning at the presence of a human being, no call that resembled the creaking of unoiled hinges ordering you to *get-back, get-back*.

Dick's spine tingled and this time the goosepimples spread right up into his scalp. The whole damned farmyard was scared to hell. Of what? Then he remembered how Ben had been last night and it was all he could do to keep his own fear at bay.

'What's the matter, Dick?' Brenda had lit the woodstove and she was in the process of cracking some eggs into a saucepan. She always sensed when he was worried, often before he was aware of it himself.

'I don't know.' He draped his jacket over a chair, reached for the mug of tea on the table. 'Right now there's not a single animal or bird out there that's acting normally. Something's frightened them, just like it did last June, the afternoon when that thunderbolt demolished that chimney in the village. Like an. . .' he hesitated, and his voice dropped to a whisper '. . .act of God, the way it was that day. Only this time *they* know about it and *we* don't. Yet!'

'You're getting as bad as Ben.' She tried to make a joke of it but it didn't sound funny and she wished she had not said it. Suddenly nothing was funny round here any more.

'How's Ben?'

'Still sleeping. I'm going to let him sleep on.'

'Well, we can't do much till this damned mist clears, anyway.' He sipped his tea, staring at the depressing greyness that eddied outside.

'The sun will be through shortly. I guess we've got to expect early morning mist from now on.'

By the time they had breakfasted the greyness was tinged with a pale golden glow, and the buildings opposite were visible. Above them the gallinis were starting to screech and a turkey stag gobbled unconvincingly in the pen.

'I'd better check that everything's ready for threshing.' Dick glanced at his watch. It was already nine o'clock.

He stopped, listened. The cattle grid in the driveway clanked and rattled.

'There's a car just come into the yard.' Brenda had beaten her husband to the window, her movements swift and nervous. 'It's too early for visitors yet, surely. Oh, goodness, it's the vicar!'

The Reverend Elmhurst was clearly agitated, an urgency about his walk, the way he rapped on the door. His chubby fingers entwined, lathering imaginary soap.

'Good morning.' He coughed nervously, the way he always did before delivering a difficult sermon. 'But it's not really so good, is it?' Talking for the sake of talking, glancing round the room as if he expected to see Ben cringing from some invisible terror.

'Whatever's the matter, vicar?' Brenda glanced at Dick. Perhaps another thunderbolt had struck the village, demolished the church.

'The. . . the *goat!*' Elmhurst's voice was scarcely audible, a croaked whisper.

'Goat?'

'Missing.' The other was trembling, clasping his hands together in anguish. 'Gone missing.'

'Gubbins!' Brenda almost shouted. 'She's been gone three days now. We've searched. . .'

'No, no!' Angry impatience, gesticulating towards the village. 'No, not your goat. The straw one, the Corn Goat. I put it in the church on my way home last night, placed it on the altar steps. . . locked the church up. Nobody's been in until this morning. Only me. The verger's away, so I've got the spare keys as well. But when I unlocked the church this morning. . .' His voice tailed off.

Dick and Brenda stared in silence, afraid of what he was going to tell them, not wanting to hear it. Praying that when he finally told them his rasping croak would not carry up the stairway, or if it did that Ben would not hear.

'It was gone!' The vicar's head was thrust forward, his neck bulging over his collar, the veins standing out on his forehead. 'Gone! Just a few wisps of straw all the way down the aisle and then. . . nothing!'

Dick Kirby turned away, stared out through the window, saw how the mist was clearing to make way for the morning sunshine. And he remembered how the livestock had been that morning. Just as he had told Brenda, it was as if they knew something he did not. And Gubbins, like the Corn Goat, was still missing. She, too, had just walked away and disappeared.

CHAPTER FIVE

Harvest festivals were always too early, Brenda decided as she sorted out two of the best sheaves for Dick to take up to the cathedral. The village were holding theirs on Friday evening, the idea devised so that the parishioners might be tempted to attend the one in the city on Sunday. Alrewas were not having theirs until the following week. Which was all rather silly when you stopped to think about it; Don Pocklington had not finished combining yet, while some of the other farmers had not even begun. So you went to church to give thanks for a plentiful crop whilst it was still standing in the fields. Anything could happen between now and the filling of the grain stores; floods, tempests, heath or forest fires that spread on to the fields. In a way thanksgiving before its time was a presumption.

'Those will do fine,' Dick grabbed up the stooks. 'I'll be back as soon as I can. Let's hope we have a good few paying customers through the gate today.'

She went back indoors, heard the Land Rover clank across the cattle grid. Her thoughts turned to Ben. He was up early for once, eating a bowl of nutty wheatflakes at the kitchen table. He looked up, nodded but did not smile. Although his fears appeared to have subsided, he was withdrawn, worrying about everything that had happened. It was a pity that he had overheard the Reverend Elmhurst's account of the missing Corn Goat. It was just another aspect of this whole illogical business to disturb him.

'Jonjo would know where the Corn Goat's gone.' He spoke quietly, staring straight ahead of him. 'Because it'll be wherever Gubbins is. And he said that Gubbins would be back.'

'I don't expect we'll see Jonjo again.' She spoke with a lack of conviction, had an uneasy feeling that before long the busker would show up. 'I don't expect he really knows where Gubbins is, he was just surmising.'

'What's that?'

'Guessing. Now, hurry up with your breakfast because before long there will be crowds of people here and we've got to demonstrate how they used to thresh the corn in olden times.'

'Maybe the goats have gone somewhere to get away from those nasty little corn men.'

Brenda sighed. 'It was a gallini you saw. And, anyway, there was only one. Now, tonight we're going to the harvest festival in the church.'

Ben's spoon clanked in his half-empty bowl, his head jerked up. 'I' m not going.'

'Why not?'

'Because. . .' He was tense, gripping the edge of the table '. . .something might happen.'

'Oh, nonsense, there will be a lot of people there, the church will be full. The Pocklingtons will be there – even Mr Pocklington leaves his work to go to the harvest festival. And you'll see Will.'

'I don't like Will any more.'

'Why not?'

'Because he's getting like his dad. He shouts and swears, loses his temper over nothing.'

That figures, Brenda thought. This conversation was getting nowhere. Firmly, she said, 'Well, you're coming to church tonight whether you like it or not. Your father says so.' Passing the buck, taking the easy way out.

'All right, but I won't like it. And I'm scared, Mum.'

'There's nothing for you to be frightened of. You can sit between us. Now, we'll have to go and get ready for the threshing.'

The threshing had been an unqualified success. Ben had helped his parents demonstrate the various methods of knocking the grain from the stooks; using a flail, treading it with the feet on the granary floor. Some seventy spectators had turned up, which was encouraging. Afterwards many of them had gone on a tour of the farm, delighting in the old-fashioned turkeys and Rhode Island Reds, amused by the gallinis which insulted them continually from the farmhouse rooftop.

But Dick was uneasy. The livestock were still edgy even after the mist had dispersed. Abby did not want to graze, but spent most of the day bleating at the field gate, desperate to return to her shed. Maybe the sheep were only after the shade provided by the tall trees in the corner of the big pasture, but they were jumpy. Too jumpy. The turkeys and hens returned to their houses in the late afternoon as if they sought safety rather than an early roost. Everything was wrong in its own small way. Only the threshing had gone without a hitch.

Ben had barely spoken all day, going about his duties in silence and with a marked lack of his usual enthusiasm. Secretly, neither Dick nor Brenda relished the coming harvest festival service; they found church-going boring, a formality that lacked its true purpose. Sure, they were thankful for the harvest and the increasing number of visitors, but the yield was way below the previous year's. Their bonus was paying spectators; that was what their business was all about. In their own way they thanked a God whom they worshipped quietly as they went about their work, eager to restore a balance to the environment which commercial farming in its greed had abused and now threatened to destroy.

Brenda was both surprised and pleased to note that when Ben came down for tea he was wearing his school clothes: black jacket and gold tie, grey trousers. He had also polished his shoes. Which meant that he was resigned to attending the service. She had feared a head-on confrontation.

She wore her grey two-piece. Suits did not seem in harmony with her husband these days. The one he was wearing tonight was the very same that he had worn to the planning office during his last few months there, yet it seemed out of place, hung awkwardly on him.

Her image of him had changed. Nowadays she never thought of him as anything other than a farmer. She would not have wanted him any other way.

'Well, are we ready?' His unease was evident. She preferred to think that it was due to the formal occasion rather than recent events.

'Yes.' She was edgy, too. 'Come on, Ben, let's go and get it over. After all, it's a good PR exercise. It wouldn't look good if the Kirbys failed to show up at the harvest festival when they're promoting everything that's good about the environment, would it?'

The village church was crowded. They managed to squeeze into a pew halfway down the aisle and then only because the other occupants squashed up to the far end. The organist was playing a slowed-down version of "We plough the fields and scatter", marking time for another five minutes. Dick's eyes roved the congregation. Don and Avis Pocklington were seated down at the front, Will in between them. Fiona and Sharon Deeps, but there was no sign of John; he was probably working, or at some conference. He wasn't the type to play a rôle in community life. Good luck to him, everybody was different.

Dick found himself staring at Sharon, remembered how she had been that day when the busker was playing, almost hypnotised by his weird music. She looked OK now. It was probably just temporary infatuation. Only then did it occur to Dick that that strange melody had not plagued him today. He could not even recall the tune. Thank God! A hesitant glance round, a sudden fear in case that busker fellow might be in the congregation. No, church services would not be his scene. More likely he worshipped some pagan deity.

The organ changed tune, the vestry door opened and the Reverend Elmhurst appeared, a pious yet imposing figure in his flowing surplice, prayer book clutched in his chubby pink hands. He turned, bowed ostentatiously to the altar, the choir behind him nodding to the gold crucifix as they passed in front of it.

Brenda thought that the interior of the church resembled an over-stocked greengrocery shop; every imaginable vegetable and fruit in season was on display alongside imported produce such as bananas and pineapples, doubtless contributed by the local schoolchildren whose parents did not cultivate a kitchen garden. With no small amount of pride she saw their own traditional barley sheaves resting against the altar drapes. Suddenly, she was glad they had come tonight. In all probability the Kirbys' offering was the only organic gift in here.

The choir filed into their stalls, the vicar paused in front of the lectern, smiled benignly. 'Good evening, everybody. It gives me great pleasure to see so many of you here tonight to give thanks for such an excellent harvest.'

Which isn't true, Dick thought cynically. Most of the farmers had not finished combining yet and those that had were disappointed with the sparse yield after the three-month drought.

'Let us begin with the traditional harvest hymn 'We plough the fields', which is to be found at the beginning of your leaflet.'

There was a short pause, maybe three seconds during which the only sound was a rustling of paper, the organist awaiting his cue. *And it was in those moments of near-silence that Ben Kirby gave a piercing scream.*

His shriek of terror was ear-splitting. Heads turned; there was a soft thump as Elmhurst dropped his prayer book so that it fluttered down the carpeted steps like a swatted night moth. Brenda jerked round, almost cried out herself as she saw Ben's face, the colour drained from his features, eyes wide and staring, a shaking hand pointing in the direction of the altar.

'Ben!'

Dick grabbed hold of his son but the child was oblivious of his grasp, ignored the sea of startled faces as he yelled, 'Look, it's back. *The Corn Goat is back!*'

Brenda followed his pointing finger, barely recognized the straw shape that nestled ignominiously amidst a row of swedes and turnips. She had not noticed it before, possibly because it resembled straw packing around the vegetables. If you studied it closely you could just about make out four legs and a head, the body plucked and tangled; there was no way that it could have stood upright without support.

Dick muttered, 'Oh, my God!' People around them were whispering, still looking towards Ben, not understanding.

'I'm sorry, ladies and gentlemen, children.' The vicar was suddenly ashen-faced, an ungainly figure stumbling down the steps, almost falling

49

when he trod on the edge of his surplice, his shaking hands gathering up the remains of the straw effigy, holding it at arms' length as though it was some obnoxious living creature that might turn and bite him at any second. 'This. . . this effigy seems to be causing some distress. Excuse me a moment whilst I throw it outside.'

Brenda heard the cleric half running down the aisle, heard the bang of the outer door. Her eyes were on Ben, saw how Dick held him, how their son was on the verge of fainting. Her own stomach heaved and she fought against a wave of nausea. This was dreadful. Maybe they should go home right now.

Ben was sitting down, his eyes opened again, and then the organist was playing the opening bars of the harvest hymn. The congregation was singing, everybody trying to pretend that whatever had happened was forgotten, that it was no more then a trivial interruption, a child's illogical phobia. Yet the singing lacked vigour, and eyes were still surreptitiously glancing towards the Kirbys.

'Let us pray.'

Brenda prayed; that Gubbins might be returned to them, the farm animals restored to normal; that Ben's corn man had only been a stray gallini. And she found her train of thought leading to that mysterious, wandering musician who called himself Jonjo. She was not certain whether or not she was afraid of him, whether she wanted to see him again.

A reading and another hymn. Ben seemed more composed now, standing up and holding his service sheet even though he was not joining in the singing. At least Elmhurst had allayed the boy's terror by throwing the Corn Goat's remains outside.

'I can smell something burning!'

Brenda heard Ben's voice over the singing, an urgent whisper. She tensed, closed her eyes momentarily. *Please, no!*

'Mum, something's on fire!'

It was! Now it was Brenda who nearly screamed as she saw a wisp of smoke rising up behind the altar. Her keen sense of smell had her nose wrinkling at the acrid stench of smouldering. Nobody else seemed to have noticed it. Embarrassment delayed her shout of 'Fire', fear that the Kirbys might be ridiculed a second time for interrupting the service. Then, before her eyes, a sheet of flame enveloped the altar cloths, licked hungrily at those dry corn sheaves below it.

And suddenly everybody was screaming.

The church was filling with thick smoke, darkening as the overhead electric lights were obscured. The congregation had begun to panic, crowding the aisle in a rush for the only exit, for the growing wall of flame was between them and the vestry door.

'Please, don't panic.' Elmhurst's cry was drowned by the screaming.

Dick had Ben in his arms, yelled to Brenda to cling tightly to them. Behind them something toppled and crashed to the floor, vibrated the pews. It was probably the lectern, knocked over by the fleeing choir. Somebody yelled that they were being crushed, children were held aloft. The vicar was shouting again for everybody to take their time, not to panic.

Everybody rushed, most panicked. But, miraculously, they all made it out into the balmy night air, spilled down to the lichgate and out into the road, a frightened crowd huddling together to watch fiery stained glass windows cracking and exploding, tongues of fire already up to the eaves.

Elmhurst stood there helplessly on the tarmac walkway, a man alone praying to his God to open the heavens and quench the fire. But the skies were cloudless, and the glow from the inferno was spreading up with the mushrooming smoke. God had, on this occasion, His own reasons for not saving His house.

Dick had lowered Ben to the ground, but the boy was still clinging to him, shaking with silent sobs. Brenda felt weak, confused, made as if to say something but her words were drowned by the sirens of the approaching fire engines. Two machines first, gleaming red monsters charging out of the late summer night, a police car in their wake. It had taken them just five minutes to reach the scene from the moment the call-out was received.

A police officer moved the crowd back on to the opposite pavement whilst hoses were unravelled, rolled out towards the nearest hydrant. Dick glanced round, saw that there was no chance of getting the Land Rover out of the church car park for the moment; he cursed himself for not having parked in the road.

A trickle of people were following the perimeter wall of the cemetery, entering through another gate. He joined them, leading Ben, Brenda following behind.

A shuddering crash came from within the blazing church and sparks showered high into the sky in a gigantic, unscheduled fireworks display. The roof had caved in; there was no hope of saving the building now. Such was the intensity of the inferno that already some of the stonework was glowing red.

Hoses swished, their foam sizzling in the flames, seemingly making no impression on this miniature volcano which erupted out of a roofless structure. Dick pressed back against the graveyard wall, felt the heat searing his face. It would be wiser to retreat into the road.

'Look!'

He felt Ben tense again, almost pull free of his grasp. Once more the boy was pointing, on the verge of another terrified scream. Shielding his eyes against the glare of the flames, Ben saw where his son pointed.

In the orange firelight a tombstone jutted starkly, eerily, out of the scorched, uncut grass, tilted at an angle as though it might fall at any second; an ancient grave, the interred long forgotten, the inscription worn smooth and illegible by two centuries of wind and rain. Grotesque if you stopped to think about it but not frightening, even to a child.

'It's only a gravestone, Ben,' Dick tried to sound reassuring, 'there are hundreds in here.'

'*Look!* ' Ben screamed. '*There, all around it!* ' Dick narrowed his smarting eyes, was aware that Brenda clung to him, both of them trying to see what it was that terrified their son for the second time tonight. Just a bundle of straw caught up against the headstone where the soft night breeze had blown it; rustling even now, wisps coming free, strewing themselves over the ground, then gently blowing on their way.

'It's nothing, Ben, just some straw blown off the stubble fields...'

'*It's the Corn Goat!* ' Ben screamed, clinging frantically to his father. '*That's what burned the church. It came back. but it was rejected, so it set fire to the church and tried to kill us all.*'

Brenda tensed. She suddenly felt very sick and it was all she could do to stop herself from throwing up. Logically, it could have been straw from anywhere, but she knew it wasn't. She sensed that Ben was right and the thought was too terrifying to contemplate.

And right now her greatest fear was that Gubbins might return as Jonjo had prophesied.

CHAPTER SIX

Canon Pilsbury had come to Lichfield as precentor on his fiftieth birthday. He was now seventy-three and still held that revered position. Retirement was out of the question; only his death would make way for a successor.

His appearance had changed little over the past twenty-three years with the exception of the greying and thinning of his hair. Short and stocky as he was, with heavy features that wore a permanent scowl, it was rumoured that even the bishop was in apprehension of his quick temper. Certainly, the choristers avoided him whenever possible and lived in dread of offending him.

On Tuesdays and Thursdays he taught Latin at the adjacent preparatory school. Parents of those pupils who attended his classes had complained vehemently to the headmaster of the precentor's mumbling speech, which their sons found incoherent, since requests by the boys for their teacher to repeat himself usually resulted in a cuff on the head, or a blackboard rubber flung with remarkable accuracy for one of such cumbersome physique and advanced years. But even the headmaster avoided the issue, fobbing off the parents with lame excuses.

Matilda Pilsbury, the canon's wife, had died fifteen years ago, a buxom woman who toured both the cathedral and the Close most days, and reported any misdemeanours by either choristers or vergers to her husband. Edward Pilsbury spoke of his widow with affection, and had told his colleagues on more than one occasion, with undisguised pride, that in all the years they had been married he had never once seen her naked.

One of Canon Pilsbury's annual duties was the supervision of the cathedral's harvest festival decorations. It was a task which he had taken upon himself in 1972, when he had complained to the dean and chapter about the shoddiness of the produce arrangement. He had volunteered then to organize it in future years and had done so ever since. Frequently he ordered Johnson, the head verger, to throw out various items of fruit or vegetables because their quality did not meet his required standards. Once, in a fit of temper, he had thrown an entire box of grub-eaten windfall apples down the north steps.

The long weeks of hot weather had not improved his temper. From the bow window of his house in the Close he watched various deliveries of produce by farmers and well-meaning gardeners. He fidgeted, eagerly anticipated his inspection, relished the prospect of his inevitable rejections. There would be several. On principle.

It was too early to go across to the cathedral yet; there would be deliveries up until 3 p.m. Anybody arriving after that would receive the sharp edge of his tongue. Hands thrust deep into his pockets, Canon Pilsbury chewed thoughtfully on nothing, an annoying habit, akin to a goat cudding, which he had developed over the years. Angry already, the thought of what he would surely find littered around the altar; people's throwouts, vegetables that had gone stale, fallen apples that were only suitable to feed to pigs. Johnson would be kept busy filling the dustbins by the north door.

Time dragged. There was a tightness around his bulky chest, he always felt it when he brooded and his anger simmered. He consulted his pocket watch, checked it against the clock on the mantleshelf. Two fifty-five. What was five minutes? By the time he had walked across to the cathedral his self-imposed deadline would have been reached.

Choir practice was scheduled for four thirty, evensong was at five. That gave him an hour and a half to reject the rubbish offerings and rearrange the harvest decorations. People had absolutely no idea how to present a scene that was pleasing to the eye. It also had to please the Lord.

Johnson was seated at the souvenir table just inside the west doors, a small, pallid-featured man with jet-black hair combed straight back. Pilsbury suspected that he dyed it, because few men at the age of forty-five could boast of absolutely no grey hairs. Vanity was a sin in the eyes of God.

'Good afternoon, Canon.' The verger rose hurriedly to his feet, shuffled a pile of booklets. 'A lovely afternoon, if I may say so.'

Pilsbury grunted unintelligibly, glowered at the other. The fellow was lazy; you always found him sitting down if there was a chair available.

'I want to check the harvest offerings!' A belligerent, mumbled demand, a trickle of spittle running down Pilsbury's chin, stringing.

'Yes, of course, sir.' Embarrassment, confusion because his duties were to supervise the sale of booklets and souvenirs, keep an eye on the offertory box at weekends when staff were reduced to a minimum. He was not supposed to leave the table unattended.

'Never mind that, Johnson.' An arm was waved impatiently.

'Yes, of course, sir.'

The verger found himself walking in the wake of the most hated man in the Close. He noted how the other shambled, wheezing because of the physical exertion and his rage. It was quite ridiculous. There was a very

54

presentable display of produce at the far end of the nave, most of which would be distributed to the poor after the service. Those old-fashioned sheaves really set the whole lot off nicely. But Pilsbury would find fault, whatever. Johnson was tense; he knew that he would be blamed.

'Hmm!' The canon wiped away his dribble with the back of his hand, surveyed the display from a distance, pushed his reading glasses up on to his forehead. There were some half-dozen tourists in the nave admiring the architecture. They conversed in whispers that echoed eerily, their tiptoed steps loud and distracting.

Pilsbury cleared his throat meaningfully, and the whispering stopped. A teenage girl halted in mid-step, then almost overbalanced as she gently lowered her foot to the floor. The canon smiled to himself, experienced a sense of smug satisfaction because his authority extended beyond diocesan employees.

'I think it's the best for many a year, sir.' Johnson voiced his opinion in the hope that Pilsbury would agree.

'It wants rearranging, Johnson, fruit with fruit, vegetables with. . .' He stopped, moved a step closer, squinted. 'What's that?'

'What, sir?' The verger's nervousness mounted, as he followed the other's pointing finger, which seemed to be directed at the pair of golden corn stooks. 'Oh, they're sheaves of corn, harvested in the old-fashioned way. There's a traditional farm just. . .'

'No, no, man. *That?*'

Johnson blinked, saw what appeared to be some kind of figurine seated between the sheaves, woven from straw, corn ears for arms and legs, balled straw for a head that was too big for the body. And a face, too, features daubed on with some kind of luminous paint that glowed in the cathedral gloom. Overall, it might have been a foot high. He wondered why he had not noticed it earlier when he had helped that fellow to bring the sheaves in.

'I think it's rather artistic, sir.' The verger saw how Pilsbury's gaze rested on him, knew that he was expected to comment. 'Sort of craftsmanship with straw, if you know what I mean.'

'It is nothing less than blasphemy, Johnson. *Who* put it there?'

'I. . . I don't know, sir. I hadn't noticed it until you drew my attention to it.'

'Johnson, you are in charge of receiving the harvest offerings. Nobody is allowed to bring anything in without your supervision. Those were my specific orders.'

'Yes, sir. Nobody has, sir.'

'They quite obviously have. You haven't been doing your job properly, Johnson!' Bulging eyes glowered, the cheeks were reddening, puffed out. And spittle was running again from those thick lips. 'You've been shirking your duties!'

'No. . . no, sir.' The verger swallowed, began to tremble. 'But I do have to sell booklets and souvenirs as well. It could be that somebody slipped it in when my back was turned. Maybe as a joke. Anyway, I think it's rather in keeping with. . .'

'Johnson, that figure which you see before you is a *corn dolly*, a symbol of pagan worship of the gods of fertility, long before Christianity. It has no place in God's house, do you understand?'

'Yes, sir.'

'Then. . . get. . . it. . . out. . . of. . . here *at once!*'

The other moved, almost running to obey. His outstretched hand brushed against one of the sheaves, stopped inches from the corn dolly as though some invisible barrier was preventing him from touching it. His eyes met those paint-daubed orbs and he flinched from them. The semicircular mouth appeared to leer evilly at him. And it was as though the temperature in the cathedral had suddenly dropped ten degrees. He shivered.

'Go on, man, get rid of it. What are you waiting for?'

'N-nothing, air.' The figure reminded him of a Punch he had once watched on the promenade at Bridlington when he was a small boy. You knew the puppet was made of wood, worked by strings, but that did not detract from its sheer evil. He had the same feeling now. Any second the thing might strike him with a vicious blow that belied its puny size. Or bite him; the mouth was a line of crosses when you looked closely, conveying sharp teeth. Its body throbbed with life, though that was undoubtedly an optical illusion caused by his own trembling from the cold and his fear of the canon.

'Pick. . . it. . . up, Johnson. Put it in the dustbin. This minute!'

Johnson's fingers moved again, closed over the tiny straw man just as he would have lifted up a slimy frog that had hopped into the cathedral. Ugh! He held it between finger and thumb, arm outstretched. A surge of dizziness caused him to sway, and his vision misted for a second or two. Then he ran, an ungainly flight that took him up the steps to the north door, fumbling it open with his free hand. He almost fell down the stone steps on the other side, went over on his ankle but somehow regained his balance. A dustbin lid clanged, bounced, and then the offending corn dolly was jettisoned inside, lying face down on a heap of dead and rotting flowers. Only when the lid was jammed back on tightly, tested with his foot, did Johnson breathe an audible sigh of relief.

For once it seemed that Canon Pilsbury had been right about the evils of paganism.

The village church had burned most of the night, only towards dawn were the fire crews able to control the blaze. The interior smouldered for most of the next day, and then forensic experts began sifting through the ashes looking for the cause of the fire. Chief Inspector Winston of the Lichfield police had not ruled out the possibility of arson. Indeed, privately, he was certain that the fire had been started deliberately.

Only a handful of visitors turned up at the Kirbys' farm on the Saturday. A catastrophe always had precedence over such bland interests as traditional husbandry.

Ben was withdrawn, and stayed indoors in spite of the warm weather. The Corn Goat had nothing to do with it, Dick emphasized until he was almost convinced himself; its reappearance was just a coincidence. They had only Elmhurst's word that it had disappeared in the first place. Vicars were generally forgetful people, engrossed in the welfare of the parish, visiting the sick, preparing sermons. In all probability Elmhurst only thought that he put the straw effigy in there on the previous night, or somehow overlooked it the next morning. Like that pitchfork which Dick had been searching for and two days later was found propped up against the goatshed wall. And Brenda's hairbrush was always going missing, usually turned up in a place where she swore she had looked previously. Whatever the explanation, there was no way that the Corn Goat could have started the fire. It could have been arson; more likely it was a fault in the electric wiring.

And there was still no sign of Gubbins.

'Somebody's coming.' Brenda had heard the cattle grid rattle, an engine slowing in the yard.

Dick spooned his last mouthful of apple pie, spoke with his mouth full. 'By the sound of it, it's a Range Rover. Don Pocklington for a guess.'

Brenda tensed. She just checked herself from saying 'He's found Gubbins' because of Ben. The church fire had been the climax to their son's escalating fears; he had slept in their bed last night, would probably do so again tonight. After the Corn Goat's supposed reappearance, Gubbins' return might have dire psychological consequences for the boy. A heavy knocking on the door boded anything but a casual neighbourly visit.

'Why, Don!' Dick feigned surprise, pretended not to notice the other's flushed features, the way his eyes blazed an uncontrollable anger.

'Your bloody gallinis are on the barley stubble!' Pocklington pointed back across the paddock. 'All bloody twenty of 'em. I saw 'em there yesterday but I thought you'd 'ave the bloody sense to keep 'em shut in after that. If they're there tomorrow, I'll shoot the buggers!'

'Oh, dear.' Dick shook his head, forced a smile. 'Don't you worry, Don, I'll. . .'

'I am bloody worried. Like I said. . .'

'Doubtless you're going to burn the stubble, then plough it in. So a few gleanings won't make a bean of difference to you.'

'I don't went 'em on my bloody land!'

'I can't shut them in, they roost out.'

'Then I'll 'ave to shoot 'em!'

'All right,' Dick was already easing the door shut. 'You shoot 'em, Don, but remember one thing, you'll have to prove damage and that won't be easy. Likewise, the corpses belong to me so you'll have to bring them here. Otherwise, it's theft. That's the law, I'm afraid.'

'Bugger the law, I'll leave 'em to burn with the stubble!'

It was as Dick closed the door that he caught a brief glimpse of young Will leaning out of the Range Rover. The boy yelled in a shrill voice, 'Get 'em off!'

'Like father, like son.' Dick resumed his seat at the table, listened to the Range Rover driving back out of the yard. 'I think maybe it's a good idea if you don't play with Will any more, Ben.'

Ben looked up, his face white. He had barely touched his food. 'I think Mr Pocklington's made the same mistake you thought I made, Dad.'

'What's that?' Dick was puzzled, suddenly uneasy.

'Those aren't gallinis on Pocklington's stubble, *they're corn men, like the one that chased me. He's taken the corn, now he's going to burn the stubble and that'll make them very angry. Dad. . . they'll kill him, just like they set fire to the church last night!'*

CHAPTER SEVEN

Canon Pilsbury had risen at 6.15 a.m. all his life, summer and winter. His strict self-discipline had not deserted him even in his latter years. One whose life was governed by routine, he put the kettle on as soon as he got out of bed, left it to boil whilst he washed and shaved. A cup of tea was poured, ready to drink by the time he had dressed. Five minutes of meditation whilst he sipped it, reflecting upon his life, remembering his departed wife tenderly, sad because she was not here to drink an early morning beverage with him. Then it was time for work.

Johnson opened up the cathedral at seven, and even when the canon was not on communion duty he checked to ensure that everything was ready for the service. On weekdays, particularly during the winter, the congregation only consisted of the Misses Evansons, elderly sisters of the late Prebendary Evanson. During the summer one or two of the resident clergy attended; Pilsbury held them in contempt for not rising early enough during the darker months. Having satisfied himself that all was in order, he would then check that the cathedral was presentable for tourists. He loathed tourists: mostly they were a godless breed who came purely out of curiosity or because they had time on their hands. Or because it was raining and they sought a place to shelter whilst the storm clouds passed. The large majority never even attended their local church whence they came.

It was humid this morning. Beads of sweat oozed on the canon's wide forehead, trickled down and smarted his eyes. He paused to wipe the offending rivulets away with a handkerchief, surveyed the Close from his garden gate. The extensive lawns had a ragged look about them, browned by the continual blazing sun, odd tufts of rye grass poking up untidily because mowing had been suspended during the drought. He made a mental note to speak to the dean later, suggest that the groundsmen clipped off those spiky stalks with hand shears. Doubtless the manual workforce had used the heatwave as an excuse to idle away the latter part of the summer.

An empty coke can glinted, caught his eye. There was a paper cup lying a few feet from it. Summer visitors added insult to injury; not content with loud whisperings and laughter in the cathedral, they left unsightly reminders of their coming. Well, Johnson could go and pick up the offending litter and. . .

Pilsbury stared, thought at first that he must be mistaken, that a pile of litter had been swept up into the corner by the old well, left there for the refuse lorry to collect. But no, it was no heap of rubbish, rather a bedraggled human figure spread out on the grass, asleep. What a darned cheek! The canon's latent anger instantly shot up several degrees, had his temples throbbing and the sweat rolling again.

The Close had been troubled during the Festival with layabouts sleeping rough on the lawns, dossers taking advantage of the fact that the police had their hands full keeping order in the city, were too busy to worry with such minor irregularities. Pilsbury had complained bitterly to Chief Inspector Winston about it and had been assured that the matter would be dealt with. It had not. So one morning he had sallied forth, nudging sleeping forms with his foot, mumbling to them to be gone. And they had refused to leave! It was incredible that such a degree of disrespect combined with torrents of obscenities could be directed at a member of the clergy, particularly a high-ranking canon. Pilsbury had called the police again and about an hour later a young special constable had arrived on the scene. But by this time the lawns had filled with breakfasting picnickers, the dossers had mingled with them and it was impossible to identify the offenders.

Pilsbury had spoken to the bishop about it but the great man himself was not prepared to take action. The cathedral lawns, he explained, gently but firmly, were there for the use of the public during the Festival; the cathedral relied upon the support and generosity of visitors and it would be not be in the Church's interests to alienate them by banning them from the grass.

But the Festival was long over now and people were discouraged from walking on the parched lawns. Canon Pilsbury shuffled forward. He would deal with this matter himself. This ragbag of a tramp would be sent packing and warned never to return here again!

The stranger's hat was pulled down over his face, just a growth of beard protruding from beneath the brim. Grubby khaki denims that went right the way down to an oversize pair of Doc Marten's, the leather surprisingly supple and polished, almost new. Probably stolen. And clutched in one of the outstretched hands was a dented harmonica. A typical hippy, Pilsbury decided, maybe one of those who came in on the so-called peace convoy that had camped up on Seven Springs back in July, lingering because Lichfield seemed to offer an easy existence for a nomad on social security. Well, this fellow was in for a rude awakening! Literally.

'Oi, *you!*' Pilsbury's shiny toecap dug into the ribs beneath the denims, twisted and pushed. The canon was starting to dribble, the saliva stringing from his mouth, a liquid pendulum.

The other stirred, groaned, but made no attempt to sit up. The fingers on the mouth organ tightened as though, in his subconscious, he feared that it might be stolen.

'D'you hear me? Get up off the grass, you vagabond!' A loud expellation of wind from the slumbering form had the canon stepping back a pace. A hand reached up, slowly lifted the hat, revealed a finely cut bearded face, dark eyes blinking open and staring up in surprise.

'I beg your pardon, sir?'

'I. . . I. . .' Pilsbury splothered, and then his words came out in an almost incomprehensible rush. 'What do you mean by sleeping here? This is cathedral property, you're trespassing. What's your name?'

'Jonjo.'

'I beg your pardon?'

'Jonjo. You asked my name, sir.' The figure struggled up into a sitting position, jammed the hat firmly on to his shock of dark hair, glanced down at the harmonica in his hand.

'Jonjo, what?' The string of saliva freed itself from the thick lips, fell to the ground.

'Just Jonjo.'

Pilsbury was perplexed. This tramp was well spoken, almost courteous. But he was a tramp, none the less, a social scrounger. Doubtless a thief, too. 'You've no business sleeping there.'

'The land belongs to the people, sir.'

'Poppycock!' Pilsbury's lips foamed, blew a bubble that burst and dribbled saliva. 'This land belongs to the diocese of Lichfield.'

'On paper.' Jonjo laughed, a strange, squeaky sound. 'Soon there will be nothing left unless something drastic is done. Man is poisoning the earth, polluting the atmosphere. His crops are loaded with poisons, except for a very few exceptions. The produce which you plan to distribute to the needy will harm them, don't you realize that?'

'Be off with you, this minute!' The canon's puffed-out cheeks were suffused with blood, and there was a sharp pain in the threateningly raised arm. 'If you're not gone from here in two minutes, I'll call the police!'

'I'll go.' Jonjo rose to his feet in one supple movement. 'Think on what I've said, Reverend.'

'*Canon!* ' There was a tightness in Pilsbury's chest now, his words barely a whisper. 'And don't you let me catch you hanging round here again!'

The canon leaned up against the old disused well, fought to regain his breath. His lungs wheezed. What a darned cheek! It was all Johnson's fault. The verger must have seen that chap sleeping there as he went to unlock the cathedral. He had ignored him, neglected his duty to the Church.

Pilsbury went in through the north door, the cool of the interior refreshing, reviving him. The pain in his arm, the constriction in his chest, subsided. Now, where was Johnson, the lazy oaf?

The canon's dragging, shuffling footsteps made a hollow echo. He coughed irritably. At the end of the nave the harvest decorations shimmered in myriad colours as a shaft of early morning sunlight slanted down on to them through an overhead stained glass window, creating a kaleidoscope effect of Nature's bounty.

Magnificent! Pilsbury altered course, embarked upon a shambling detour, his anger momentarily forgotten. Such beauty demanded appreciation. In a few minutes the sun would have moved round, he might never see the harvest offerings in such splendour again. Absolutely superb, truly one of God's gifts to Man, the very source of life itself!

He stood there, head bowed, murmuring a prayer of thanksgiving. And then, in one awful moment, his reverie was shattered and he was recoiling with a grunt of fear and anger, the stabbing pain back in his arm.

The corn dolly was back. sitting there between the pair of barley sheaves, its posture an undisguised arrogance.

This was impossible! It wasn't, because the effigy was there, right in front of his frightened eyes. But it was somehow different this time. He swallowed, his Adam's apple bobbing up and down, seeming to swell in his throat, threatening to choke him. *For the corn creature's features were more than just daubs of luminous paint; they had assumed a lifelike appearance that was terrible to look upon. Eyes that glinted malevolently, saw and understood, a mouth that was twisted into a hateful leer. And its expression was focused upon him. There was no doubt about that.*

Pilsbury backed away, lost his balance and almost fell, unable to tear his gaze away from that terrible inanimate caricature that watched his every movement. His chest was hurting again; it was difficult to breathe.

'Johnson! Johnson, help me!' Pilsbury did not know whether he had actually uttered that cry for help; there was a roaring in his ears that deafened him. He tried to tell the thing that he meant it no harm, that his orders for it to be removed were all a mistake. He hadn't realized that it was *alive*.

Trying to apologize, his lips moving, his chin wet and shiny with spittle, but the tiny corn man was not fooled. *You have insulted a god mightier then yours, one upon whom the fate of civilization rests.*

The canon nodded, blasphemed his agreement, pleaded for mercy. It was all a mistake, he had no idea. It leaned forward, pointed accusingly at him. *Mankind will perish because of fools like you.*

'Canon! Canon Pilsbury, are you all right?'

Pilsbury felt a supporting hand on his arm, recognized Johnson's voice, almost wept his relief except that a verger was no match for Satan's messenger, no more than he himself was.

'Look!' He croaked, pointed with his free hand, cowered before the terrible effigy, its image now just an indistinct shape through his blurred vision.

'Oh, my God!'

In any other circumstances Pilsbury would have remonstrated with the verger for taking the name of God in vain. Johnson held him tightly, and he felt the other stiffen.

'You see what I see, Johnson?'

'Yes, Canon.' Johnson's voice quavered. 'The corn dolly. . . I don't understand. . .'

'But *look* at it, man. Its face. See how it moves and. . . and *lives!*'

'I. . . beg your pardon, Canon?'

The man was a fool. One did not expect a high level of intelligence from a verger but surely he was capable of seeing.

'It's *alive*, Johnson.'

'I'm afraid I don't understand you, sir.'

God forbid! 'Johnson, just look at it. See its face, its expression.' Pilsbury discovered that he was able to move his head, stared down at the carpeting because he feared to look upon that countenance of sheer evil again.

'It looks just like it did yesterday to me, sir.'

'No, *no!* It can see, move, speak. . .' The canon risked a glance and this time his reaction was mingled relief and disbelief.

For the corn dolly was just as it had once been, its features crudely painted, blobs of paint for eyes and nose, a line of crosses for teeth.

'I. . . I don't understand.'

'Let me help you back home, sir. It's the heat, you know. It can do funny things to you.'

'Thank you, but I'll be all right, Johnson.' The pain was gone again. His breathing rattled but apart from that he was just weak and frightened. And angry.

'Johnson, I ordered you to throw that. . . *thing* out yesterday.'

'Which I did, sir. You watched me carry it outside.' The verger's neck prickled. He would never forget how that repulsive little creature had seemed to move in his grasp. 'I put it in the dustbin.' And I jammed the lid down as hard as I could in case it. . . escaped.

And it had escaped.

'Perhaps we were both mistaken, Johnson.' Please tell me that you had

63

second thoughts and brought it back inside after I'd gone. And maybe it was the heat that made it seem the way I saw it. He wiped his brow with the back of a flabby, trembling hand.

'Maybe somebody looked in the dustbin, saw it lying there and thought it would look nice amidst the harvest decorations, Canon.' That was the logical solution. Wasn't it?

'Yes, yes, that's what happened for sure, Johnson.' Pilsbury allowed himself to be led away from the nave, leaning heavily on his companion.

You. . . you don't want me to throw it out again, do you, sir?' A note of fear, pleading.

'No, absolutely not!' Pilsbury's reply was emphatic, loud enough for its echoes to carry all the way back to the altar. Just in case that corn man *was* alive and was listening. 'I think I was rather hasty, Johnson. It was the heat, of course. In fact, I think it's rather nice, sort of a good luck charm. Without us worshipping false idols, that is. An exhibition of corn craft.' He laughed, had to force the sound. Then, suddenly, his mood changed. 'Oh, yes, there's another matter I have to take up with you, Johnson.'

The verger's stomach churned. He was experienced enough to detect a reprimand, a forthcoming rollicking. 'Oh! What's the problem, Canon?'

'What time did you unlock this morning?'

Johnson swallowed, knew better than to lie. 'I was a trifle late this morning, Canon.' He failed to stop a nervous gulp. 'Maybe ten minutes, no more. I overslept.'

'Quite, quite.' Now it was the canon who gripped the verger by the arm. 'Johnson, did you not detect anything unusual as you walked across towards the west doors?'

'No, sir.'

'Nothing at all? Was there nothing by the well that attracted your attention but because you were late you decided to overlook it? Eh?'

'No, sir. Oh, you mean a couple of items of litter on the lawns. Yes, I did see them but I thought I'd retrieve them when I popped back home for my break. After all, there's not going to be anybody about until just before communion, is there?'

Canon Pilsbury's vision swam for the second time that morning. The hand that gripped the other, and was the forerunner of a rebuke, now held on for support. 'You're *quite* sure, Johnson? You didn't see anybody sleeping on the grass?'

'I'm absolutely sure. I looked around in case there was any more rubbish thrown about. You know how these kids like to sit on the well, drink cans of pop and throw the empties on the lawn. Well, I know I looked there in particular.'

'I see.' The canon was trembling violently. 'I think perhaps I will get you to see me home, Johnson. As you said, the heat can do strange things to you. Sometimes you see things that aren't really there.'

As they emerged through the west doors, Pilsbury found himself glancing fearfully around. There was no sign of the tramp, thank goodness. But through the pounding of his head and the roaring in his ears, he detected a faint sound. It might have come from down by the Minster Pool or over from Stowe Pool. Or from Beacon Street or Gaia Lane; its direction was impossible to guess. It swirled in on the faint morning breeze, a weird, lilting melody that the brain picked up and retained, played over and over again.

'Do you hear music, Johnson?'

The verger cocked his head to one side, listened intently, shook it slowly. 'No, Canon, I can't hear anything.'

'I must have been mistaken,' But he knew he wasn't as the rhythm increased to maddening proportions. And it was with a frightening sense of realization that Canon Pilsbury recalled the battered harmonica that the man who called himself Jonjo had clutched in his hand. The other's words came back to him: that prediction of doom for the world, and how the corn man, too, had warned of man's embarkation on a path of self-destruction.

CHAPTER EIGHT

Abby, the white saanen goat, objected to being milked. She had never given any problems before and Dick Kirby was puzzled. Her bucket of feed was knocked over, concentrates scattered across the floor of the small milking parlour. She pulled to the extent of her chain, kicked.

'Damn you, what's the matter?' He grabbed her collar, hauled her back into place, decided that he would have to milk one-handed, restrain her with the other. His left knee was embedded in her flank; she wouldn't be able to move now.

He heard pellets bouncing on the floor like the contents of a pack of frozen peas spilling out through a slit. Goats always had a means of protest in waiting. That was the first; the second caught him by surprise.

The animal squatted, sat down on the milking bucket, trapping his fingers against it. He cursed, and snatched his hand away, and the fast stream of urine jetted into the milk, its sour odour rising with the steam.

'Blast you!' He stood up, tried to pull her away, succeeded in knocking the bucket over. Abby continued to urinate, turning her head and regarding him with an expression of smug satisfaction.

He let her finish, waited for her to stand up, and then, by sheer brute force, finished milking her, squirting the remnants of her udders on to the floor. You always had to win in the end where animals were concerned. Abby had fought him all the way but ultimately she had been milked against her will. The fact that there would be no fresh goat's milk for breakfast was of secondary importance.

'Having problems?' Brenda appeared in the doorway of the parlour, and regarded the flooded floor with dismay.

'Yep. Like every other creature on this place, Abby is playing up, which means we'll be having powdered milk in our tea and let's hope for better luck at evening milking. I don't suppose there's any sign of Gubbins.'

'No.' Brenda shook her head. 'Somehow I get the feeling that we've seen the last of her. But we've got another problem.'

'What now?' Dick paused in the act of squeezing out the mop. 'No, don't tell me, Don Pocklington has shot some of the gallinis.'

'Wrong,' but she did not smile, 'the gallinis haven't left the yard today. I'm afraid it's the Barkers' horses. Two of them have broken through into the meadow.'

He glanced heavenwards, sighed. 'Give me a couple of minutes to mop up and then we'll go and drive them back through wherever they got in.'

'I wouldn't go into the meadow if I were you.' There was a flicker of unease that bordered on fear in her eyes. 'They're going crazy, Dick, tearing up and down, eyes rolling, frothing at the mouth. They'd trample you to death just for the hell of it.'

'Maybe they've been bitten, or stung. An adder, perhaps.'

'Both of them? That's most unlikely.'

'True.' He was thoughtful. 'I'll give Tom and Rita a ring. Or go round.'

'I've tried both. They're not at home.'

'In which case their bloody horses will have to stop in the meadow until they get back.'

'They're chasing the sheep. Scaring the hell out of them, too.'

'Jesus Christ!' He leaned up against the wall. The Barkers had been a nuisance ever since they had moved into the derelict stables just down the road. In an unintentional way, of course; just thoughtlessness fuelled by their blinkered obsession with horses. Shortage of money was Tom and Rita's problem; they could not afford to repair their rotting fences so the horses were always getting out. They didn't tax either the horse lorry or the Land Rover, left the former parked on the side of the road so that it caused an obstruction. Miraculously, the police had not noticed it. Their well had long run dry so they were forced to fetch water in drums from the Sheets' farm on the other side of the village. Dick had had to stop supplying them with water in case his own borehole ran dry. Pocklington was too mean, wanted to charge them for it. All in all, the Barkers were a pest.

'I'll have a go.' Dick put the mop back in the bucket.

'No, please.' Brenda grabbed him by the arm. 'You've no idea.'

'Don't worry, darling.' he kissed her. 'I'll go in the Land Rover. That way I should be able to drive them out through the gate.'

'On to the road?'

'It'll have to be. Anyway, we don't get many cars along this stretch, and maybe the horses will go back down to the stables once they're on the road.'

'I suppose so.' She wasn't convinced. 'At least Ben seems a lot better today. Quite cheerful, in fact. He's gone for a walk up the fields.' She was unable to hide her concern.

'He'll be okay. Look, the animals are edgy too; it's probably just the weather. As for the fire in the church, if it's arson then the police will conduct an enquiry. More likely it was an electrical fault. That business over the Corn Goat was, I'm certain, just the vicar's absentmindedness. And that fellow Jonjo appears to have left the area, so we can't blame him. Before long the weather will change and everything will be back to normal.'

'I suppose so.' Brenda did not believe him, knew that he didn't believe it either. The whole countryside was going crazy.

The horses, huge black shires, were up at the far end of the meadow. The sheep had scattered and were bleating plaintively. Dick climbed out of the Land Rover, opened the gate, pulled it wide. The horses saw him for the first time, stood watching. There was something about their posture that was odd, disconcerting, the way they tensed like coiled springs, heads lifted. Any second they might break into a charge.

He bumped the Land Rover on to the tussocky grass, decided on a detour that would bring him behind them. That way they should drive easily enough, just like sheep or cattle running in front of a vehicle. Once they saw that the gate was open they would surely head directly for it. They had only broken out of the Barkers' small field because there was no grass for them to graze. In all probability they were hungry. Short of water, too.

He drove slowly, and they watched him all the way, ears erect. Their stance was threatening, almost as though it was they who were herding him, waiting for him to reach the point where they wanted him. His mouth was dry, his instinct to wind the window up in spite of the heat. The sheep were crowded into the opposite corner, milling in unmistakable terror.

The horses moved, surprisingly slowly, and in the direction in which Dick had intended. They sensed freedom through the open field gate. He accelerated a little, not enough to alarm them, just enough to bring him to within twenty or so yards of them in case they veered off.

Fifty yards from the gateway, they stopped. He braked, rolled to a standstill. Their tails were flicking, and in one graceful movement, as if their animal intuition had synchronized the movement, they wheeled round towards him. That was when he saw their faces, and mentally recoiled. Eyes that rolled in crazed fury, nostrils snorting like angry dragons. Damn them, they had had no intention of going out through the gate. Their co-operation had been nothing less then a cunning ruse to trap him in the field, cut off *his* escape route.

He slammed the gears into reverse, but there was no way the vehicle was going to outstrip the speed and strength of those horses. From a standing start they came at him, one on either side, rearing up, hooves poised to smash through the flimsy canvas roof of the Land Rover.

The engine gave its own roar of defiance, and somehow the Land Rover dodged the first assault, careering backwards, swerving as it hit a bushy tussock, enough to cause the attacking shires to misjudge their aim. Hooves clattered on steel, dented the bonnet, caused the horses to slip and roll. Then they were up again, neighing their anger at having been foiled.

Dick slammed into bottom gear, roared forward, took his attackers by surprise and went straight between them. Now it was himself who was heading for the exit, the horses in pursuit. They caught him up, galloped alongside, but they had not the balance to allow them to strike a moving object. They dared not intercept it, aware that the ton of mobile steel was capable of causing them serious injury.

Racing on either side, perhaps they hoped that the engine would stall. There was no way of understanding equine minds. Teeth gripped a strip of trailing canvas, there was a loud ripping noise and part of the soft roof was torn away. Dick accelerated, bounced crazily; the gate seemed no nearer.

The horses were crazed with rage, screaming. One was level with the cab, attempting to push its head inside. The glass was smeared and he had a close-up view of wicked teeth. If he overturned, they would drag him out, bite and kick, roll on his unprotected body. He had never liked horses. He suddenly remembered something his father had once said: 'Horses bite with one end, kick with the other.' It was true enough.

The gateway, thank God! One of his pursuers was almost crushed between the Land Rover and the gatepost, somehow slewed and twisted out of the way. The Land Rover burst through, shot into the road. Fortunately there was no passing traffic or else a serious accident would have been inevitable. He hit the opposite verge, and the vehicle lurched, threatened to overturn, somehow remained upright. Two wheels churned the dried grass, the others gripped the tarmac as he made a right hand turn. Fearfully, he glanced in his wing mirror, saw to his relief that the maddened creatures had given up the chase, were standing there in the entrance, lathered in sweat, just watching him. He had shown them the way to freedom and they had spurned it. Whatever attraction the meadow held for them, they were unwilling to relinquish it.

In the distance he saw an approaching vehicle. At first he thought it was a service bus, then he recognized the blue and red hand painting that had obscured the vivid yellow of a former county library van. Tom and Rita were returning in their dilapidated, converted horse lorry. Well, they had better bloody well do something about rounding up their straying animals. Dick pulled up in the road opposite the parked lorry, saw Tom Barker's shiny bald head behind the wheel, Rita's mop of deep chestnut hair beside him. They wore T-shirts, looked hot and sweaty after an excursion to some gymkhana in their unlicensed vehicle.

'Hi, Dick!' Waving, carefree, climbing out of the cab.

'Two of your horses have broken through into our meadow.' Dick Kirby had to call upon every vestige of restraint. 'They're going crazy, chasing the sheep. And they've just ripped a piece out of the Land Rover's canvas!' He leaned out of the window, pointed to the damage. 'And they've put a couple of dents in the bonnet, too.'

'That'll be Oscar and Bobbin, for sure,' Rita smiled, 'their energy is inexhaustible. They're *so* full of beans.'

'I'll get them.' Tom leaned back into the truck, withdrew a couple of halters. 'No problem. Rita, put some oats in a bucket.'

'Don't be a fool,' Dick snapped. 'They've gone mad. Either it's the heat or they've been stung. They'll kill you if you go near them!'

Tom and Rita Barker appeared not to have heard him as they busied themselves to catch their escapees. A halter each, a bucket of bait. They did not anticipate anything more than their routine for catching strays.

'They'll trample you to death, roll on you,' Dick shouted after them as they began to walk back down the road, 'they're kill crazy. Look what they've done to the Land Rover!'

But the Barkers were not interested in vehicular damage. All that mattered was that Oscar and Bobbin were unharmed. They did not hurry; you only panicked horses by showing undue haste.

'On your own bloody head, then!' Dick yelled after them. 'And you owe me for a new canvas and bonnet!'

The Land Rover stalled, and he had difficulty in starting it again. The carburettor often flooded in hot weather. Damn the Barkers. They couldn't afford to repair their fences and the odds were that they weren't insured, either. He'd end up footing the bill. Happy-go-lucky horse freaks always muddled through in their own infuriating way and got off scot free. And they'd whistle that pair of crazy nags and they'd come trotting home as if they'd just been for a canter down the lane!

The engine roared. He revved to make sure that it didn't cut out again, and moved out into the road. He'd have to go up to the Barkers' entrance to turn round. It was too narrow here.

God, what a mess! He tried not to see inside the stables yard but it was impossible to overlook it. A litter of straw and empty paper feed bags, equipment lying all over the place. The house was probably worse, but you could bet your bottom dollar that the stables were immaculate. A dog of indeterminable breeding was doing its business on the concrete walkway from the house. That made a change: usually it sniffed its way down the road and did it on the Kirbys' small roadside lawn. God, give me goats and sheep any day!

He was fifty yards from the open gateway to the meadow when he heard screams above the noise of the Land Rover. Shrill yells of terror that mingled with the neighing of horses. He braced himself, jammed the accelerator pedal down on the floorboards and prayed that he would get there in time. Even if he did, he had no idea what he would do.

He didn't, which probably saved his own life, a third needless casualty amidst a bloody equine rampage of flying hooves and slashing teeth. Any rescue attempt would have been futile from the outset.

The shires were in the process of rolling on the battered corpses of their owners, legs flailing skywards as they flattened and spread the scarlet mulch, screaming their sadistic glee, their glossy coats a patchwork of claret and black, and only when they had cracked every last human bone would their maddened lust be appeased.

Dick turned his head away, drove shakily and erratically back home to phone the police. Only then did he begin to search the house and farmyard for Ben.

Ben had wandered up the steep rough track that overlooked the barley stubble. Inexplicably, his fears had subsided as if somehow he sensed that he would be safe on his parents' land. Because the corn was harvested, gone, it could no longer conceal tiny figures that shrieked insatiable lust and chased after children.

Pocklington had not beaten his own self-imposed deadline for the completion of combining. Because the early morning mists meant a delayed start to the day's work, the grain was not dry enough to cut until mid-morning. There were still some fifteen or twenty acres of corn standing, barley that had been sprayed with innumerable harmful chemicals invented by Mr Deeps, the agrochemist, who lived in the big house on the edge of the village. Those nasty little men wouldn't like it in the Pocklingtons' barley, Ben thought, chuckling, but he hoped they would stay there. He wondered what would become of them when the harvest was finished. Perhaps they would go and live in the deep woods for the winter, somewhere snug and warm like Hopwas Wood to the east.

He had been awoken by gunfire early this morning, about an hour after daylight when the countryside was enshrouded in thick autumn mist. Dad had said it was Don Pocklington venting his frustration on the gallinis which had strayed over the boundary in search of gleanings for breakfast. But Ben knew it wasn't the guineafowl because they were still screeching in the yard after the sun had broken through. All twenty of them. It was the corn men Pocklington had been shooting at. Ben's sympathies were mixed. Both deserved their comeuppance.

He reached the brow of the hill, followed the hedgerow down alongside the stubble. He wondered if he might spy Gubbins somewhere. Perhaps it was better if she did not come back. He remembered only too well the consequences of the Corn Goat's return.

'Hello, Ben!'

Strangely, Ben did not jump. He barely tensed as he turned around slowly to confront the bearded figure with the floppy hat pulled down

71

over his face to shield his eyes from the glare of the sun as he surveyed the patchwork of fields laid out below. Jonjo appeared to be searching for something amidst the parched pastures and hedgerows.

'Gubbins hasn't come back,' Ben stated, almost accusingly. 'You said she would.'

'She will, she will,' Jonjo smiled whimsically, 'but it is early yet. I promise you she will return when the frosts come.'

Ben nodded, believed him. 'She won't set fire to the farm, will she?' he asked anxiously.

'No!' Jonjo shook his head, 'Rest assured, you and your parents, and your livestock, will be safe. It is the others who are at risk.'

'Like Mr Pocklington?'

'Perhaps. Who knows?'

'Have the little corn men gone, Jonjo?'

The busker did not answer, concentrated his gaze upon the distant skyline where a bright yellow combine harvester gobbled a wide swathe through the golden barley. He seemed to be watching for something but the distance was too great to see clearly.

'I'm frightened of the corn men, Jonjo.'

'They only harm those who destroy the food supply upon which they depend,' the other replied without turning his head. 'This season they are enraged because the danger has never been greater. Sometimes they make a mistake but afterwards they are sorry.'

Ben did not understand, but something warned him not to enquire further. He fidgeted, feeling uneasy and embarrassed because he was imposing upon the other's solitude.

'There has been an accident .' Jonjo spoke in a whisper, perhaps unsure of whether he should tell this innocent child. 'Two people have died.'

'Oh!' Ben felt slightly sick. 'Not. . . not another fire.'

'No. You see, it isn't just the corn men, it's the animals, too. They are just as sensitive to what is happening to the environment. They are edgy, frightened. Sometimes they panic and then they are not responsible for their actions. Just as man is not on occasions. But you'd better go, Ben. I fear that your parents will be looking for you.'

Ben had already begun to walk away when Jonjo called after him. 'Ben, perhaps it is best if you do not say that you have seen me.'

'All right, Jonjo.'

'Promise?'

'I promise.

'Good boy. Now, don't worry because everything will come right in the end. As I told you, Gubbins will return with the frosts and you and your folks will be fine. But there is a long way to go yet and time is running out. Now, go on back to your parents.'

Ben stumbled back down the steep path, confused, but no longer afraid for himself and his parents because Jonjo had assured him that they would be safe. And the busker would not lie.

CHAPTER NINE

Fiona Deeps had sat in front of the television for the last three hours but the moving images, the garbled dialogue, had not registered with her. She thought the news had been on earlier but she could not be sure. A film: she had no idea what it was or even what it was about. She had fidgeted on the leather Chesterfield sofa, crossed and uncrossed her legs; she wasn't sure how many Bacardis she had drunk. Certainly enough to push her over the limit if she needed to use the car. And it was all her husband's fault.

Fiona had been adamant that Sharon was not going to the disco at the community centre. There were innumerable reasons why she had vetoed the idea, instigated a screaming match with her daughter. The fire in the church for a start; they had been lucky to get out alive. If there was an arsonist at large then the centre was a prime target, packed with teenagers, the exits inadequate even if they had been passed by the safety authorities. And these local discos *always* ended with a fight. A few weeks ago a youth had had to have fifteen stitches in his face because some lout had smashed a beer glass in it. There were other reasons that had emerged in the row with Sharon. Some of the more disreputable lads, living off social security, were on the lookout for vulnerable girls. There were already two under-age pregnancies in the village, and good-class girls always saved themselves for marriage. A twinge of guilt here at the hypocrisy, but it was for a good reason. She herself had become pregnant out of wedlock (that was *entirely* John's fault, but at least they were engaged; it was merely a question of bringing the wedding forward) but she most certainly would not have agreed to casual sex. One had to have principles, morals, and it was her duty to protect her daughter from temptation.

'You can't stop me from going!' Sharon was already dressed to go, wearing that dreadful revealing frock and plastered in cheap make-up. 'I'm going whether you like it or not!'

'I shall lock you in your room!'

That was when John had come in from his study, irritated by the disturbance. 'For God's sake, Fi, all kids go to discos. It's part of growing up. And, damn it, it's only just down the road, it's not as though she's going into the city!'

Two to one. Fiona had conceded with bad grace, a parting shot as her daughter hurried out of the house before her father changed his mind, 'You're to be home by midnight even if the disco doesn't finish till one.'

Naturally, Sharon wouldn't be back by midnight, on principle. Fiona wished that her husband had stopped over in town tonight, so she could have sorted the problem out to her own satisfaction. John wasn't around when he was needed and on those occasions when he wasn't, he was present. Sharon had inherited her stubborn and rebellious nature from her father, never mind all this balderdash about kids growing up.

Fiona glanced at the clock on the wall. Twelve thirty. Realistically, she had to give her daughter another half hour, say ten minutes after that to walk home. If there was no sign of Sharon by one fifteen then she would walk down to the community centre and fetch her back. She got up, crossed unsteadily to the cocktail cabinet and poured herself another Bacardi. It helped, and, anyway, she wouldn't be needing the car.

Tonight was the first instance of outright teenage rebellion that Sharon had shown since. . . since she had wandered off to listen to that busker. Fiona had only just realized, and it was disconcerting. A kind of barrier had arisen between daughter and mother from that very day; the frequent arguments and rows had faded unobtrusively, to be replaced by an absence of conversation, Sharon keeping to her room, only showing up at mealtimes and not talking even then. She avoided direct questions, however trivial, her replies mostly grunts or nods. It was eerie.

Even the fire at the harvest festival had not jerked the girl into either shock or terror. It had been Fiona who had been on the verge of panic. Sharon had filed quietly outside, seemed almost unaware of the danger.

Twelve forty-five. Fiona stood up, began to pace the lounge. She resisted the urge to refill her glass; she might need a clear head shortly. And John was still out there working in his hermit den, he couldn't give a monkey's. Well, Sharon was his responsibility, too, and it was up to him to go down to the centre and look for her.

Fiona left the room. The passage seemed to lurch like a cabin cruiser that had hit a choppy stretch of water. She held on to the knob of the panelled door at the far end, waited for the floor to steady before she entered the room with its fluorescent lighting that seared her eyeballs.

The interior was a combination of office and laboratory: floor to ceiling windows, workbenches that reminded her of the chemistry and physics room in her schooldays. A desk littered with sheets of paper, a PC, cork notice boards on which were pinned numerous charts, tables and coloured diagrams. God, it stank in here, stale cigarette smoke combining with sharp chemical odours to conjure up disturbing thoughts of all the cancers you had read about and a few you hadn't.

'John!'

A balding head lifted at the desk, the expression taking a few seconds to adjust to the untimely interruption, showing its annoyance.

'What is it, Fiona?' Sharp tones, reprimanding her for daring to disturb him.

'Sharon's not home yet.'

A sigh of annoyance, as he consulted his watch. 'But she won't be back for another half hour, at least.'

'I told her she had to be home by midnight.'

'Well, she's not going to take any notice of that, is she? The disco doesn't finish till one, and mostly they go over. Allowing for kids hanging on, chatting outside, I wouldn't really expect her back before one thirty at the earliest.'

'John, I want you to go and fetch her home. Now!'

'I can't right now. I'm just finishing an analysis which needs to be handed in at the lab tomorrow. It's a breakthrough if it works.'

'You're a director now, not a bloody chemist.'

'I am an agrochemist!' There was a distinct note of pride in both his tone and his expression, a hint of fanaticism. 'If the world is not to face starvation, then chemicals are vital in producing the necessary food supplies. Herbicides and pesticides are an integral part of modern agriculture. Weeds and pests must become a thing of the past if sufficient food is to be grown. Time is not on our side.'

'You mean you poison the starving so that there's enough left to go round the survivors!'

'Stupid woman! I can see you've been talking to that fellow down the road, the traditional farming freak!" he retorted.

'I've never even met him. I don't need to; I know what's going on even if you lot are blind to it. Money is all you care about. You think more of poisoning the environment than you do of your own daughter.'

He sat down again, turned his back towards her. 'Call me if she's not back by one forty-five.'

Fiona went out, slammed the door behind her.

Back in the lounge the ceiling seemed to spin, steadied and stopped. She'd be all right, she'd have to be, and in any case she wouldn't need the car. She had to stare hard at the clock face before the time registered. Twelve fifty-five. It was time to be gone.

There seemed to be a lot of nocturnal activity in the village. A horn blared from a passing car and some youths shouted obscenities out of the window. It was obviously turning-out time at the disco. Sharon ought not to be mixing with this type of youth, she would be better off in some sort of intellectual society in the city.

The community centre was lit up and a crowd of teenagers were congregated in the doorway. Fiona wrinkled her nose in disapproval of their attire, outrageous punk clothing and multicoloured haircuts. They were watching her approach too closely for her liking; it made her apprehensive. She hoped that Sharon was not amongst them.

'Excuse me,' she addressed the gathering, nobody in particular, 'I wonder if any of you have seen Sharon Deeps?'

'Sharon *who*?' A weedy-looking youth in a black jacket spoke. 'Sharon *Creeps*, did you say?'

The others laughed, nastily. Fiona drew a deep breath, wondered why there wasn't a policeman around. She thought the police were supposed to check all such events. 'Sharon Deeps. D.E.E.P.S.'

'Never bloody 'eard of 'er, missus, let alone seen 'er. Wouldn't know 'er if we did.'

They all laughed again and Fiona strode haughtily past them into the hall. The stench of body odours and spilled beer was almost overpowering, the shiny wooden block floor awash, litter strewn everywhere. Some men were collecting chairs, stacking them in piles, a disc jockey was busily dismantling his equipment.

'Excuse me.' There was a hint of panic in her voice now. Clearly Sharon was not here.

'Nobody's allowed in 'ere after one, lady!' A man with a crew cut, wearing a sweat-soaked T-shirt that revealed the contours of his bulging beer belly, regarded her with hostility. He belched loudly as though to emphasize his words.

'I'm looking for. . .'

'Everybody's gone. Just us left to clear up.' He turned away, picked up another chair, jammed it on the top of an already precarious stack.

Fiona rushed back outside. The punks had left, except for a couple necking up against the wall. For one moment she feared, hoped, that the girl was her daughter. She would grab her arm, drag her all the way back home! It wasn't Sharon; this girl was overweight and could not have been more than fourteen at the most.

'Sod off, missus!' The boy turned, spat on the ground.

Fiona started to check the piece of rough ground that served as a car park but there was no lighting. She stumbled in a pothole, almost fell. Tears welled up in her eyes. Oh, where are you, my darling? Please let me find you. I won't be angry now. *Please.*

Everybody had drifted away, just the neckers left behind. Fiona gave way to a sense of futility, sheer hopelessness. It's your fault, John, you selfish bastard! If you'd listened to me then Sharon would be safe at home in bed. Now she's gone and we'll never find her.

A pair of headlights were turning into the main entrance, tyres crunching on gravel. The car stopped, sidelights only, engine ticking over.

'Can I help you, madam?' The voice sounded authoritative, and along the side of the vehicle her strained eyes made out the word POLICE.

'Oh, thank God! Officer. my daughter's missing. She was supposed to be here but. . .'

'I wouldn't worry, madam.' The policeman made no effort to get out of the car. 'The village is full of kids going home. Boy and girlfriends lingering the night out, going somewhere for coffee. If I were you I'd go on back home and I'll bet you when you get there she's waiting for you. Nothing to get worked up about. If there's no sign of her by morning, then give the station a call.' He let in the clutch, flicked the headlights back on, and drove out through the gateway.

'My daughter's in trouble, I know it,' Fiona shouted after him but the revs drowned her words. That was when she surrendered to her emotions and burst into a flood of tears. And amidst her sobs she heard again the weird harmonica music that had almost driven her crazy a few days ago. Now it grated back, had her clutching at her ears in an attempt to shut it out.

It was nearly dawn before John Deeps finally accepted that his wife's fears were well founded. For the past few hours he had put forward innumerable possibilities concerning their daughter's whereabouts. She was in a tantrum after her mother's unreasonable demand that she didn't go to the disco so she was deliberately stopping out all night just to get her own back.

'But *where*?' Fiona shouted hysterically. 'She doesn't know anybody, she hasn't got any friends because we only moved in here a few weeks ago. You tell me where she might have gone, John!'

'With a boy, probably.'

'That's ridiculous. Sharon wouldn't stay out all night with a *boy*!'

John Deeps thought better of pointing out that teenagers today were more mature, physically and mentally, than they had been in his and Fiona's day. If Sharon was still a virgin he would be surprised, to say the least. 'Probably a gang of them are sitting in somebody's lounge drinking coffee.'

'That would be preferable to a lot of alternatives,' Fiona replied tearfully. Her sobs shook in time to the rhythm of the mouth organ's melody inside her head, and in her mind she saw again that dishevelled, bearded busker, and Sharon's near-hypnotic expression as she listened to him playing; the way she had been since, withdrawn and brooding. That possibility was too frightening to contemplate.

At 7.30 a.m. John Deeps phoned the Lichfield police and reported that his daughter was missing.

By ten o'clock the police were conducting a house-to-house enquiry throughout the village. Nobody who had been at the disco, it seemed, had any recollection of seeing a girl resembling Sharon Deeps' description. Detectives worked on the theory that the girl had not gone to the community centre on the previous evening, that she might have had an alternative destination or, worse, been abducted en route.

An hysterical Fiona provided them with a recent black and white photograph which would be copied and circulated to other police forces. If she was not found by this evening then her picture would be shown on television and in the *Evening Mail* and the *Express and Star* in the hope that somebody's memory might be jogged.

Whilst Sharon's distraught parents waited by the telephone for news of their missing daughter, police with tracker dogs, aided by a platoon of recruits from the nearby barracks, methodically searched Whittington Common, Hopwas Wood and Cannock Chase. Isolated pools were checked by frogmen and a helicopter aided the searchers.

Today the thick mist had been reluctant to disperse as though it hid some guilty secret. It was 11 a.m. before the sun finally broke through and the surrounding villages were aware that a girl had gone missing. The villagers recalled other similar disappearances over the years, all with tragic consequences, and they feared the worst.

Up on a scrubland hillock on the outskirts of the village, a lone watcher followed the progress of the searchers. As the sun approached its zenith, he pulled the brim of his wide, soft hat down to shade his eyes from the glare. He lay in a patch of bracken, seemed impervious to the swarm of black flies which buzzed around his head and settled all over him. He made no attempt to swat them, his only movement an instinctive caressing of the scratched and dented harmonica which dangled from his neck.

He watched out of curiosity simply because he happened to be in this place, having slept away the night hours on a snug bed of undergrowth. The shouts of a searcher who thought he had made a discovery, which turned out to be the illicit burial of a dead ewe by some lazy farmer, had disturbed him. Jonjo decided that it might be imprudent to reveal his whereabouts so he remained where he was until the long line of beaters were tiny specks in the far distance. Only then did he unobtrusively slip away, resisting the temptation to play his mouth organ until he was out of earshot.

CHAPTER TEN

Canon Pilsbury had rested throughout the day prior to the commencement of the harvest festival service in the cathedral. He had dozed fitfully in his worn and shiny leather armchair, his study/ living room a cool refuge from the fierce midday heat. Once the telephone had shrilled but he had let it ring on, too lethargic to get up and answer it.

Towards late afternoon he stirred, went through to the kitchen and brewed a pot of strong tea. The beverage revived him somewhat, so that he almost relished the prospect of the forthcoming service. Of course, all that business this morning was a combination of the heat and his age. He had imagined those features on the corn dolly. Its return was undoubtedly some prank played by a mischievous tourist. Possibly that busker fellow. But *he* had been sent packing, he would not return.

The canon was not due to go across to the cathedral for another half hour. Johnson would be supervising the final preparations, the distribution of service leaflets and prayer books. In the meantime Pilsbury would watch the early evening news on television; it was vital to keep up to date with current affairs, which nowadays played a major part in the Church's policy. In recent weeks there had been a move afoot to ban field sports on all Church-owned land. He had supported it in a sermon. Unfortunately, the voting had gone against the motion; he failed to understand why the synod condoned the killing of God's creatures.

The news was just starting, headlines about a coach crash on the M1 and a Midlands girl who had gone missing. Pilsbury offered a silent prayer for the relatives of the dead in the former, and that the injured might recover.

'A fifteen-year-old Midlands girl has now been missing for almost twenty-four hours.' The newscaster's expression was grim. 'Last night, at around eight thirty, Sharon Deeps walked to a disco in her home village near Lichfield in Staffordshire.'

The canon stiffened, leaned forward, his interest and concern aroused. A television camera followed a route that was well known to him. He had once presented awards to the boy scouts in that very community hall.

'It is not known whether or not Sharon arrived at the disco. Her concerned mother went to look for her at around one a.m. and there was no sign of her. Police and soldiers, aided by civilian volunteers, have spent the day combing the surrounding countryside. This is a recent photograph of the missing girl and anybody who might have seen her after eight thirty last night should telephone the following number. . .'

A black and white photograph of Sharon Deeps appeared on the screen. Canon Pilsbury stared, just in case he might have known her at some time. It wasn't likely. He did not pay much attention to youngsters; modern youth was a godless generation.

His fourteen-year-old set crackled, wavy lines denoting a tube that was in need of replacing. He would only do that when it actually expired. The screen went fuzzy, distorted like a funfair house of mirrors. Sharon's picture elongated to ridiculous proportions, stretched her features into a ridiculous caricature.

And that was when Canon Pilsbury gave a cry of terror, jerked back in his chair, a flabby hand pressed to his chest; a moment of agony in which he almost blacked out, seconds of acute pain in both his chest and his arm as his angina reacted to the sudden shock.

For in those awful few seconds recognition hit him with the force of a physical blow. The cartoon-like features of Sharon Deeps bore an undeniable likeness to the corn dolly that had glared at him with such malevolence that morning, that effigy which had seemed to come alive.

The screen blurred, faded, returned with a report on an athletics event. The canon closed his eyes, was relieved to feel his pain subsiding. His body was bathed in sweat and he was trembling violently.

It was all due to heat and stress. Such a likeness was laughable, an impossibility. There was no way there could be a link between a straw doll and a missing girl; the two were totally unrelated. His pulses raced, his head throbbed, and in the depths of his confused mind he seemed to hear again that harmonica music. He thought it sounded like 'Greensleeves' but he could not be sure, was only too relieved when it faded away.

He sat there, dozed again briefly. Some minutes later he stirred, feeling surprisingly refreshed, as though he had slept deeply for hours. He determined that he would attend the harvest thanksgivings. There was no earthly reason why he should absent himself.

As he donned his surplice he found himself wondering if that corn dolly would still be on the altar in its arrogant posture between the corn sheaves. It surely would be, for it was an inanimate object and he had instructed the verger to let it remain.

This evening one of the assistant vergers would be on the west doors minding the sales table for Johnson's duty was to remain in the Chapter House. The St Chad Gospels were on show to the public, the most intriguing of Middle Age manuscripts, rumoured to be worth more than the Mappa Mundi in Hereford cathedral, pages of inscribed and decorated vellum. Eight of them had survived since before the tenth century, believed to be of Oriental origin, perhaps Coptic.

They had been on show during the Lichfield Festival, guarded by a special constable throughout their display. The canon thought it foolhardy to risk them again for the harvest celebrations but the dean had been adamant. 'They are a major public attraction,' he had put his fingertips together, a habit of his when he was immovable in his determination to have his own way, 'and with costly restorations in process we need to attract every visitor we can. Agreed, the Gospels are a risk, they always will be. Some unscrupulous foreign collector would pay a fortune for them on the antiques black market, just to have them locked away in his private museum. And, in the past, there have been threats by animal rights activists who would deface them because they are made from animal skins, albeit over a thousand years ago. But they will be well guarded, and after the harvest festival they will be locked safely away again.'

The cathedral was already filling up with regular local worshippers and tourists who were enjoying a late summer break in the city. They thronged outside the west doors, queuing for admittance, marvelling at the architecture, the statues above the archways, St Chad flanked by twenty-four kings. There was an atmosphere of celebration which, Pilsbury grudgingly admitted to himself, was only right for the occasion, thanking God for a bountiful harvest.

The interior of the cathedral was sombre, its coolness refreshing. As he made his way towards the vestry, he checked that the verger was in the Chapter House. Johnson was there, thank goodness, standing with his hands clasped behind his back, seemingly the epitome of dignity and knowledge. Some tourists were conversing with him in loud whispers, doubtless enquiring about the history of the Gospels. Pilsbury just hoped that the verger would not make a fool of himself. His knowledge of the subject was scanty, gleaned from the guide book.

The canon briefly checked on the array of produce, sighed with relief when he saw that the corn dolly was still there. From a distance, and with his poor eyesight, it had the appearance of having wilted, a limpness in keeping with most of the leaf vegetables. It certainly was not alive now. Nor had it ever been, if you thought about it logically.

Ten minutes later the long, winding procession of choristers, deacons and clergy filed into the nave, bowed as they passed the altar, took their places in the stalls. The nave was full, people were standing at the back and along the sides. A full house always created the right atmosphere, the canon thought as he knelt briefly. Yet he sensed a feeling of expectancy, tension even, from the congregation. It was probably in his own mind, a niggling residue of recent happenings, real or imaginary. Or maybe they remembered the fire in the village church, were dwelling on the disappearance of Sharon Deeps. Pilsbury tried to push both from his mind but they refused to go.

He mimed the words of the first hymn. He was not up to singing tonight and, anyway, his voice would not have been heard amidst the hundreds of others. With the exception of the choir, the singing in the cathedral was always subdued, doubtless brought about by awe in this magnificent place where humility was a virtue.

Everybody knelt for prayers and an address by the dean. There was more coughing than usual from the congregation. Pilsbury was convinced that some of them did it on purpose, or at least made no effort to control it. Nervousness and boredom were the main culprits; some were attracting attention to their presence here, making sure that they were noticed. For them it was a social occasion; few really entered into the true spirit of worship.

'Let us now say together the Lord's Prayer.'

It was at that moment that a piercing scream echoed throughout the cathedral. Picked up and magnified by the tannoy system, it reached a terrifying pitch and was taken up by women and children. Worshippers were panicking, stumbling out of their pews, congregating in the central aisle, huddling together.

A sudden, awful silence in which everybody seemed to freeze for maybe three or four seconds, trying to believe that it was all a mistake, that the public address system had screeched, nothing more. Everybody was looking round, some of those at the rear had slipped out through the door. Just in case there was going to be another fire.

A prayer book fell somewhere, hit the floor with a resounding *thump.* A child squealed, clung to its mother.

The dean had moved away from the lectern, seemed uncertain of where to go, where to look for the source of the cry. Canon Pilsbury shuffled from his seat, instinctively bowed to the altar as he passed it. And that was when he recoiled, staggered back, would have screamed, too, if his intended shriek of anguish had not become trapped in his throat. His lips moved soundlessly and he started to dribble, peering through a scarlet-tinged mist of blurred vision. His thick neck bulged over his collar as his head moved to follow the trail of wisps of corn straw that led down the altar steps and away towards the Chapter House. His gaze retraced its shaky course, fixed unbelievingly on the empty space between the two corn stooks. He closed his eyes, opened them again, prayed that it might have been a trick of his failing eyesight, an optical illusion. But it wasn't.

The corn dolly was missing.

He panicked, stumbled in the wake of the dean, an ungainly shamble that somehow caught the other up.

'It seemed to come from the Chapter House.' The dean might have been talking to himself, slowing his pace because he was afraid of what he might find there.

Pilsbury did not reply, kept close behind the other, instinctively using him as a shield. Their dragging footsteps made an eerie, hollow sound; everybody was watching but nobody followed them. Dean, Canon, go and look, tell us who it was that screamed. And why.

The dean halted outside the entrance to the Chapter House, hung back. Canon Pilsbury heard his sharp intake of breath, his gasp of despair. Fearfully, he peered round his companion, grunted his own dismay at the confirmation of his worst fears. He pressed his sweaty hands to his eyes to shut out the scene, again praying that it was all a mistake, that it had not really happened. It could not be, it was impossible. Johnson had been on guard the whole time, a loyal servant who would give his life for the Church if that ultimate sacrifice was required of him.

Finally, the canon had to accept that it was reality, that this act of sacrilege, this vandalism, had indeed happened. From their respective frames the Gospels hung in fraying, tattered ribbons, strips of ragged vellum, torn patterns that resembled carnival streamers and buntings, wafting gently as if to mock the watchers.

'No!' the dean rasped, wrung his bony hands together. 'Please, God, no!'

Pilsbury's eyes had shifted from the desecration, stared transfixed at the floor, saw the scattered litter of straw, a mocking reminder of that Christmas time when the Chapter House had been decorated as a manger, had been a holy shrine where visitors came and looked piously at the Christ child in the crib.

Now, surely, it belonged to Satan himself, the trail of straw that led from the altar littered by demoniac hands, a stench as though beasts of the wild had made their lair in here. And so bitterly cold that you found yourself shivering uncontrollably.

Two pairs of frightened eyes roved that exquisite Chapter House, afraid of what they might see. Dean and canon pressed close against each other seeking comfort and protection from some inconceivable horror, and finally they both screamed together. Clasping each other tightly like devoted brothers in torment, their cries bringing a tiptoeing army of nervous feet to share their trauma.

And suddenly it seemed that everybody, the entire congregation, was screaming. For, lying amidst the straw, was Johnson, the head verger, staring up at the roof with open, unseeing eyes that even in death reflected the sheer horror of whatever had struck him down.

CHAPTER ELEVEN

Avis Pocklington had learned over the years to ride out her husband's uncontrollable tempers; the one and only point in his favour was that he had never hit her. She still cried, but she tried not to let either him or Will see her in tears. Whatever went wrong in the house or around the farm was invariably blamed on herself. It would never be any different. She had, of course, contemplated leaving him on more than one occasion. She wouldn't miss him, no way, but why should she give up her home, relinquish her share of the farm which she had helped him build up from one smallholding? Sure, half would be hers, but it wouldn't be worth the hassle. Will was another reason why she had stayed. And her son was growing just like her husband. She consoled herself with the promise that as soon as Will had finished his schooling, then she would be off, maybe get herself a flat in the city and really start to enjoy life. In the meantime. . .

'Where's our tea, then?'

Avis did not turn round from the sink, continued washing dishes, slowly and methodically stacking them in the rack. She glanced in the mirror, saw Don framed in the doorway, his narrow face flushed with the deep red of anger, his thin lips curled in contempt.

'You said you were going to work right through, finish the combining and have a late cooked supper.' She spoke evenly, no trace of resentment in her tone.

'I didn't. I only said it was a *possibility*!'

'All right, I can have something on the table in twenty minutes.' She ought to have learned by now that he contradicted himself almost daily, changed his mind over something several times a day, and expected her to know instinctively of his change of plans.

'You're a thick cow!' He stepped into the kitchen, left the door ajar behind him. Through the gap she could see Will out on the step, listening and grinning to himself. 'I'll bet you've been sat in front of that television.'

'I watched the news.' There was neither annoyance nor resentment in her reply, just a statement of fact.

'Bugger the news!'

'There's a girl in the village missing, in case you didn't know.' This time her tone was heavy with sarcasm. 'She's the daughter of an agrochemist, without whom you wouldn't be able to spray the weeds and pests on the crops. He's probably earned you an extra fifteen-per-cent yield on the grain.'

'There'll always be others to make pesticides and herbicides. They don't rely on one man.'

'That doesn't alter the fact that his daughter's been missing for almost forty-eight hours. She's probably been raped and murdered by some pervert, her body dumped where it won't be found for weeks.'

'Look, how long are you going to be with the bloody tea?' His shout bordered on a scream, and he advanced a step towards her.

'You don't care about what's happened to her, do you, Don?'

'I bloody don't. I've got a crop of grain to combine.'

'Neither do you care that the Barkers got kicked and trampled to death by their horses.'

'We won't miss them. Nor their bloody nags always getting out into our fields.'

God, she really hated him now, her hands clenched out of sight beneath the surface of the soapy water. She said, 'There's been some trouble in the cathedral last night. The St Chad Gospels were vandalized, slashed to ribbons, and the head verger was found dead at the scene.'

'He probably slashed 'em then cut his own throat.'

'I don't think that's very funny. Actually, he died from a heart attack, probably brought on by trying to stop the culprits.'

'I'm sure all that will make a lot of difference to me. Now, what about this tea?'

Avis heard Will sniggering outside. She fought back her tears, wondered why some fancy man hadn't stepped into her life. Other women seemed to find them easily enough. The reason was simple: the only time she went off the farm was on Thursdays when she went into Lichfield to do the shopping. She had even stopped going to church because Don forbade her. 'Like I said, Don, twenty minutes. Longer now because you've delayed me.' She caught her breath. It was the nearest she had come to answering him back for years, and on the last occasion he had locked her out of the bedroom and she had fallen asleep sitting on the landing.

'You can stuff the tea then!' He kicked the door in his rage, slammed it back against the stop.

'I'm starving,' Will whined.

'Then you can bloody starve! We're going to finish that barley tonight if it takes us until daybreak. And another thing.' He leaned round the door, dragged out a rusty old 12-gauge hammergun which was propped

87

up in the corner, reached down a handful of cartridges off the shelf above. 'I reckon those bloody gallinis of Kirby's will be in the grain in the late evening. I missed the buggers last time. I won't tonight! And it's a pity 'is bleedin' goats don't do to 'im what the Barkers' 'orses did to them!'

The door slammed shut and Avis let her tears come. She would be forty next month, and was still reasonably attractive; young enough to find herself another man. And this time it was no idle promise made to console herself.

Don Pocklington switched on the combine's headlights with the approach of dusk, their twin beams piercing the misty gloom, showing the rich golden grain. Another half hour and the harvest would be finished. Gripping the wheel, he stared at the last of the standing corn, tensed as a ripple ran through it. It might have been the night breeze, but he knew it wasn't.

'Those bloody birds are in there!' he yelled to Will, but the boy did not hear him above the roar of the machine. Don reached down, picked up the shotgun, cradled it across his chest with his free hand. Those gallinis were in for one helluva shock. They wouldn't fly, they'd leg it towards the nearest hedge like they usually did. With luck, if he blasted into the middle of them with both barrels, he might kill half a dozen.

He turned, went back down the centre of the field. Another turn, just one swathe left, and in the headlights he could see the barley bending, parting, as something scuttled on ahead of him. He slowed deliberately, not wanting to flush them out of range.

'Dad, did you hear that?' Will cupped his hands, used them like a megaphone to make himself heard above the vibration.

'Can't hear a bloody thing, boy.'

'Sommat's screaming in there, screeching like it's hurt or angry.'

'Your ears are better than mine. It's them gallinis. You wait a minute and you'll see something worth watching!'

'Didn't sound like gallinis to me.'

Stupid boy. You wouldn't hear the gallinis over this racket even if they were squawking. He's getting as daft as his mother.

Any second now. Don Pocklington slowed the machine to a crawl. Fifteen yards. Ten. Just a small clump left, the buggers were huddled in there. Move, or I'll bloody cut you to ribbons! He let go of the steering, gripped the gun in both hands, clicked the hammers back.

The very last patch of corn burst into life as a bunch of scattering figures were flushed, strange shapes in the deepening dusk, scampering to the left to avoid the blinding beams of light. Two-legged, about a foot high, they *might* have been guineafowl with wings outstretched so that they resembled arms.

'*Dad...*'

Will's shriek was drowned by the crashing double report, and he was blinded momentarily by the twin stabs of flame from the end of the barrels. The recoil threw Don backwards, and he almost lost his balance.

'Got a couple, surely. Go pick 'em up, boy. Your mother can feather and dress 'em.'

But young Will Pocklington did not move, stood there clutching the safety rail of the platform, his pallid features turned towards his father. There was no mistaking his expression of terror, the way he was struggling to speak, his lips moving but no words coming from them.

'Well, what are you waiting for, bloody Christmas?' Don's outstretched hand rested on his son's chest, threatened to push him overboard.

'Dad. . . those. . . *those weren't gallinis!*'

'Don't talk bloody nonsense. They were Kirby's birds stealing our grain. Now, go and pick 'em up. At least we'll 'ave somethin' out of that freak!'

'*No! They were. . . little men!*'

'You'll get a clip round the ear in a minute. Now, go. . . and. . . fetch. . . 'em!'

Whimpering, Will descended the ladder, fell the last two rungs and sprawled headlong on the spiky stubble. He started to cry. The figures he had glimpsed before the gunflashes had blinded him were like grotesque dwarfs, shaggy miniature humans that squealed with rage and fear as they fled. He was frightened of what he might find out there but he was even more frightened of his father.

'Hurry up, are you bleedin' blind? They'll be out there, about ten yards to your right.'

There was nothing there. Will walked the area in cross sections, following the frantic waving of his father's arms.

Don cursed, began to climb down. The boy really was as thick as his mother, no two ways about that. 'I'll find 'em, you stand where you are.'

But there was nothing to be found, no limp and lifeless corpses lying in the stubble.

'You must've missed, Dad.'

'I don't miss, boy. I was knockin' down partridges on the wing when I was your age. They must be wounded, made it as far as the hedge. Too dark to find 'em now. Still, that's taught Kirby a lesson. Come on, let's get back. By now that stupid bitch might just've got the tea on the table!'

They climbed back up on to the platform, swung the combine harvester round in a circle, rumbled towards the far gateway, the headlights cutting a path through the gathering darkness some hundred and fifty yards ahead of them.

'Dad, there's somebody sitting on the gate!' Will shouted, pointing.

Don Pocklington stared, made out a figure perched on top of the five-barred aluminium gate. 'Now who the hell can that be? If it's Kirby lookin' for his birds then he'll go home with a bout of earache!'

But it wasn't Dick Kirby, Don could tell from the silhouette. The fellow wore a wide-brimmed hat, was too lean for their neighbour. The farmer drove into the gateway, killed the engine and let it shudder to a halt.

'Who the blazes are you, and what d'you think you're doing sitting on my gate?'

The figure did not move, just sat there, a featureless outline in deep shadow.

'Did you bloody hear what I said, feller?' Don's groping fingers found the gun lying on the floor, lifted it up with a threatening gesture.

'I heard.' The voice was low and cultured. 'But I don't care for your language, sir.'

'I don' t give a. . .'

'This track,' the stranger pointed to the path leading up to and through the open gate, "is a public right of way. If you don't believe me, consult an ordnance survey map where you'll see it marked. I checked it before I came up here.'

'A funny bugger, eh?' Pocklington cocked the gun. This guy wasn't to know that there were only spent shells in the chambers. 'Well, my gate isn't for the public to sit their asses on, so you can get right down this very minute!'

'If you really object.' The other jumped down in one perfectly co-ordinated movement. 'I apologize for sitting on your gate, farmer.' Something oblong and silver dangled from his neck. 'I was merely surveying the landscape.'

'Then go and survey it somewhere else.' Don lowered the shotgun, then his tone changed. 'I don't suppose you've seen any gallinis around?'

'Gallinis?'

'Guineafowl. Grey birds about the size of a pheasant, make a helluva noise.'

'No, sir, I've seen nothing at all. Good night to you, farmer.'

Don Pocklington's hand shook as he restarted the combine, over-revved the engine. A little shiver had begun at the base of his spine, prickled its way right up to the nape of his neck. A moment of fear that passed as quickly as it had come, and he would not have admitted to anybody that he had been afraid.

But for some inexplicable reason, the unknown man on the gate, whose face had been shrouded in shadow throughout their brief encounter, had terrified him.

CHAPTER TWELVE

Don Pocklington's mood had tempered now that the last of the barley had been combined. He also savoured the satisfaction of having put a double charge of lead pellets into Kirby's gallinis. Of course he had hit them, there was no question of missing, he had probably wounded three or four, maybe more, condemned them to die a lingering death in the hedgerows. There would be no point in looking for them next day because the foxes would have found them at daybreak.

'And if I find that bloody goat he's lost wandering about on our land, it'll get the same!' he told Avis and Will at breakfast the following morning.

Avis did not reply, winced as Will laughed. The boy was not pursuing his theory of 'little men' rushing out of the last patch of standing corn. When Don's mind was made up over something, nobody changed it. All the same, the boy's laughter was nervous, he was clearly ill at ease. Avis decided that his drawn features and black-ringed eyes were due to sleeplessness rather than working long hours. Another disconcerting thought crossed her mind. Young Ben Kirby had rambled on the last time he had been here about a little corn man who had chased him. It was probably all kids' fantasies, nevertheless it was slightly worrying.

'Well, we want to get all the baling finished before the weather breaks.' Don pushed his chair back, stood up, spoke through a last mouthful of toast. 'There's no time for sitting around at the breakfast table.'

'The *Country File* forecast on Sunday said there was no sign of rain in the coming week.' Avis began to gather up the plates.

'I don't take any notice of weather forecasts.' her husband was already on his way to the door. 'I can tell 'em more about the weather than they'll know in ten years, in spite of all their fancy computers and the like.'

After she heard the tractor leave the yard, Avis went through to the living room and switched on the television. Don went berserk if he caught her watching TV at any time other then late evening. 'If you've got nothin' to do, I'll find you a job,' he had sneered on countless occasions. But she had to know if there was any news on the Deeps girl.

There wasn't. Avis consoled herself that no news was good news. On the other hand, kids that went missing were usually dead within the hour. There was an extended local news bulletin; police and soldiers,

91

aided by civilian volunteers, were today combing Gentleshaw Common. Door-to-door enquiries had now been extended into Lichfield city itself. John and Fiona Deeps were 'bearing up, sitting by the telephone waiting for news'. It was always the same: parents clutched at straws until those straws were snatched from their grasp.

The police believed that the desecration of the St Chad Gospels was the work of animal liberation front activists although the organisation had not yet admitted the outrage. Johnson, the head verger, had died from a heart attack, doubtless brought on by the shock of seeing the priceless Gospels shredded before his eyes.

So far there was no conclusive evidence to prove either that the church fire was arson or that it resulted from an electrical fault. The police were keeping an open mind. Tomorrow Tom and Rita Barker were being buried.

Avis switched off the television, went back into the kitchen and began washing the breakfast dishes. There were just too many catastrophes lately for her to believe that they were coincidences. She tried to dismiss Will's story of little men from her thoughts. It refused to go.

'I really don't think Will's well enough to carry on baling.' Avis failed to keep the apprehension out of her voice as her husband got up from the tea table. She despised herself for her weakness; she had been rehearsing her argument since lunch. 'Will's not going back up the fields, Don. He's got a headache, he isn't well. It's the hot sun that's done it.' She wasn't used to speaking forcefully, demanding. 'He'd better go to bed. It's after half past seven already.'

'Work never hurt nobody.' Don Pocklington glanced at his son contemptuously. 'Makes men out of boys. There's many a time I get a headache, I just don't tell nobody.'

You bastard, she thought. 'Well, I can't see him being fit to work tomorrow if he carries on now.' It sounded weak, pleading on Will's behalf. The boy was resting his head on his arms, looked hot and flushed. 'You don't feel well enough to go, do you, Will?' Passing the buck.

He did not reply, scared to say that he felt ill.

'Please yourself.' Don jammed a nylon baseball-type cap on his head. 'Don't complain when your pocket money's short at the end of the week.'

He stalked off, slammed the door so hard this time that it rattled the crockery on the table. Avis rested a trembling hand on Will's shoulder. 'You go on up to your room, Will. See how you are tomorrow.'

'Mum,' he raised his head and she saw how his eyes were wide with fear, 'those weren't gallinis last night. They were little men, and they were very angry.'

92

'All right, they were little men.' Even as she told herself that she was humouring him, already there was a nagging doubt in her mind. 'Don't you worry about them. They won't come into the house, they'll stop out in the fields.'

'Mum?'

'What is it?'

'I'd like to play with Ben again.'

'There's no reason why you shouldn't.' She stroked his cheek affectionately, felt how damp it was.

'Mr Kirby's got it right, you know. It's Dad that's got it all wrong. You can't go on poisoning the land like that. And when Dad burns the stubble, the smoke will blow down into the village and folks will breathe it in. It's like passive smoking.'

'I think you're right, Will,' she said in a hushed whisper, 'but I don't think either of us had better tell Dad so.'

Later on, after Will was asleep in bed upstairs, Avis Pocklington cried.

That boy's a bloody wimp, Don Pocklington told himself as he baled the straw frantically, the baler shuddering and vibrating under the strain. He'll never be any good on the farm and he doesn't have the brains to do much else. Thick, like his mother.

He left an untidy trail of straw bales in his wake. Tomorrow Will would work, in health or sickness, probably the latter. He'd have to stack the whole field, pile the bales into blocks of eight ready for carrying. Work until he dropped in the hot sun, that'd bloody teach him to shirk. This time tomorrow he might really be feeling ill, and serve him right.

Don only baled the big field, enough straw for their own needs, the rest would be burned on the ground, the sky a smoky red glow as far as you could see. There was no money in straw, the bales weren't worth the twine it took to bind them. So you set fire to the fields. And if this slight breeze kept up then that was great because it would blow the smoke towards the village, suffocate the bastards, and in particular whoever it was who had reported Will to the police for driving the tractor. Interfering buggers. They'd no idea what farming was all about, how their food reached the table. Fortunately, Don had been let off with a warning but he would have to be very careful about letting the boy drive the tractor from now on. Which meant a loss of cheap labour. Nobody was any good on a farm if they couldn't use a tractor. And the last thing Don Pocklington wanted was to pay a workman's wages.

It might have been the Kirbys who had phoned the police. Just the sort of thing these play-farmers from the city would do to get one up on a *proper* farmer. Traditional farming, my ass! Farmers had an ever-increasing population to feed, and it would be impossible without chemicals and advanced techniques. Farming was all about progression, not regression.

The baler groaned its protest at a bale that had jammed. Cursing, Don leaped down, gave the offending straw rectangle a kick. The machinery clanked, carried on where it had left off. Ten minutes later he had to do the same again. Maybe they were due for a new baler. He never troubled to turn it off whilst he rectified a jam, that way you lost time. The safety authorities wouldn't agree, but they didn't have to make their living at a job where time was money. They just wasted your time checking on you with their stupid book of rules.

It was dusk already. Don was determined to finish the field even if it meant working by headlights. Two or three times more up and down should see to it. Yes, he would get a new baler next time, one that worked faster. An agricultural loan would take care of it, an added bonus being that it was tax deductible.

Blast it, the baler had jammed again. Don hit the ground at a run, raced to the rear of the tractor, climbed up on to the shuddering machinery and kicked at the offending wedge of straw. *And then he screamed because his boot had become trapped in a tangle of baler string, the plastic variety that only snapped under extreme tension.*

He tried not to panic even as the obstruction freed itself, began to move into the thumping baler. He pushed a shaking hand into the pocket of his trousers, felt for his knife. One slash and he would be freed. His fingers scrabbled through a filthy handkerchief, some loose coins, gripped the lining, tugged it inside out. *Oh God, the knife wasn't there.*

The baler jammed again, compressing a wad of straw, and the bale which held him stopped moving towards the shute. Don was sweating profusely, shaking with terror. There was still time to free himself. Perhaps his knife was in the other pocket, or the hip one.

It was not in either, but so long as the line of bales didn't start to move again he would escape. Perched precariously on his uneven foothold, he tore at the string with trembling fingers. It was in an unbelievable tangle, a kind of cat's cradle around his instep and heel, knotted. He tore at it, grunted with pain as the artificial fibre cut into his flesh. *Please don't start working again.*

And that was when he first saw the semicircle of huddled figures some ten yards away, little more than silhouettes in the deepening dusk, watching him intently. Kirby's bloody gallinis had come to mock him in his plight! Except that there was something about their stance, their shapes, that was not somehow identifiable as guineafowl. Their outstretched wings were too narrow, more like arms, their coats too rough and shaggy for feathers.

He stared into the gloom through eyes that smarted from his pouring sweat, heard an echo in his tortured brain, recognized Will's voice. *Those weren't gallinis, Dad, they were little men.*

Stuff and nonsense. There was no such thing as little men except in fairy story books. OK, they're not gallinis, something else then. Pheasants, or some of those crazy rare breeds escaped from the traditional farm. Or animals. Hares! That was it, father and mother hare had brought their litter to watch a man trapped by agricultural machinery, a rare treat for the creatures of the field.

'Bugger off !' He shouted at them, screamed as the baler jerked, stopped again. He wondered if he could get his boot off. He pulled back, grunted loudly. But there was no way his tight-fitting footwear was going to slip off his foot.

His tiny audience shuffled closer. Now he could see them more clearly, and he almost fainted. *Will had been right, they were tiny men, roughly made human caricatures, fashioned out of straw, and they even had tiny grinning faces, features that leered evilly at his plight.*

It was some kind of sick joke, he told himself. Kids from the village had been up here, had made some corn dollies, set them up so that they looked real, their movements caused by the faint breeze. He couldn't waste any more time with whatever they were; he had to escape before the baler decided to work again. He should have switched it off as the safety authorities advised. It was too late now.

There was no way he was going to be able to break the twine or remove his footwear, he had to accept that. The sweat on his body had chilled and he was shivering, heard his teeth beginning to chatter like castanets.

'*Help me. Please, help me!*' His cry of despair was addressed to the eerie gathering, the vulture-like figures that were regarding him with undisguised sadistic glee.

They began to laugh, shrill titterings that escalated to a high-pitched shriek, waving their ragged arms in the air, moving their feet in some kind of nightmarish death dance.

And suddenly the baler was moving again; chugging, vibrating, Don Pocklington's trapped foot going into the chute with the straw. He began to scream hysterically, struggled in vain. There was no way he was going to prevent his body from being compressed into a chunky square of scarlet mulch. His vision began to darken, mercifully spared him the sight of those impish creatures scuttling forward, climbing nimbly up on to the vibrating machine in order to view his demise.

As his consciousness ebbed from him, he heard, above their shrill, excited cries, the lilting sound of a mouth organ somewhere, slowly playing him out.

CHAPTER THIRTEEN

'There are some questions I'd like to ask you.' Detective-Sergeant Hampson of the Lichfield CID closed the door of the interview room behind him and regarded the outlandish denim-clad figure seated at the table. He decided that this might well be a lengthy session, pulled up a chair and sat down.

Hampson was in his mid-thirties, with short-cropped fair hair and a ruddy, lived-in face. His approach being abrupt to the point of rudeness, he was a favourite in the local force for interviewing stubborn suspects. This guy might prove awkward, a cross between a hippy and a diddicoy by his appearance.

Hampson laid a clipboard out on the table, studied it whilst he lit a cigarette. Mrs Deeps had remembered her daughter listening to this fellow busking in the market square, recalled how she seemed almost hypnotized by him. There were further reports of his being seen in the city and its surrounding countryside. Kirby, the organic farmer, had seen him around the farm, didn't like the way their son idolized him. Just a common vagrant or a pervert? A potential sex-killer? The sergeant would know soon enough.

'Name?' He fired the question with the suddenness of an ambusher's shot.

'Jonjo.' The reply was instantaneous, almost casual.

'Jonjo what?' He was obviously a cool customer, had maybe been interrogated by the police before. Hampson would check him out afterwards.

'Nothing else. Just Jonjo.'

'That's crap. Everybody has a first and second name.'

'I never did, sir.'

Their eyes met. Jonjo's gaze was unwavering, almost disarming.

'I see. Any fixed address?'

'None.

'You sleep rough, then. Vagrancy is an offence, you know.

'I'm not a vagrant. I only stay where I am welcome.'

'Where've you been staying around here?'

'I've slept on common land. There is no law against that.'

'True, but I want to know where you were on these dates. . .' Hampson reeled off the evening when Sharon Deeps had disappeared, the church fire, the desecration in the cathedral. The Barkers' and Pocklington's deaths were accidents, just coincidences.

Jonjo pulled a creased and tatty large scale ordnance survey map from his pocket, spread it out on the table. The policeman leaned across, saw that there were crosses marked; Whittington Common, Cannock Chase, Hopwas Wood, Gentleshaw Common, dates scribbled against them.

'What d'you keep these records for?' Suspicious of an alibi. The busker would have nobody to corroborate his overnight outdoor dossing places.

'My diary. I travel the entire country and this is the easiest way of recording my itineraries.'

Shit, there was no way of proving or disproving the other's answers. You got a hunch when a suspect was telling the truth, and the detective had one right now.

'I see.' He stubbed out his cigarette in the ashtray. 'Let me see that thing.' His hand reached out, pulled the harmonica towards him, held it at the full extent of its cord. Silver, scratched and dented. He made a note of the hallmark. Later, he might, or might not, check on its country of manufacture. 'Hmm.' He let it go, it swung back against the other's chest. 'You were busking in the market square. Twice. Once when Mrs Deeps and Kirby saw you. And this afternoon when the patrol car picked you up.'

'That's right.'

'You need a licence.'

'I don't have one, I'm afraid. But if you tell me where I can purchase one, I will get one today.'

'I'll find out and let you know.' You didn't threaten minor prosecutions when you were hunting a possible child killer. 'Where were you born?'

'I have no idea. I was abandoned at six months, found in a public convenience and spent the next sixteen years in an orphanage. In Leeds. Maybe I was born in Leeds, I don't know.'

'Means of support?'

'I don't draw social security, neither do I beg. People give me things. A meagre reward for my playing. I shall be pleased to purchase a licence.'

Hampson lifted up the questionnaire sheet, lifted a passport-sized photograph from beneath the clip, thrust it at Jonjo. *'Ever seen her?'*

'Why, yes.' A brief smile; the dark eyes flicked up from the picture, met the detective's. 'She was in the crowd the first time I played in the city. I remember her because she kept moving through the throng until she stood right by me. I haven't seen her since.' Which took care of the next question.

The detective took his time lighting another cigarette, replaced the photograph. 'She's missing, we have to find her. Fast.'

'Oh, dear, I'm sorry. I hope that you find her safe and well.'

'So do I. Now, what are your immediate plans. . . Jonjo?'

'I plan to stay around this area. Until the first frosts, anyway.'

'What's the significance of the frosts?'

'Cold nights. I shall then go somewhere warmer.'

'A large city? Subways, underpasses, a dosshouse, eh?'

'Perhaps. As I said, I have not planned beyond the frosts.'

The policeman tried not to show his irritation. There was no way he could hold the busker, he had to let him go. 'I guess that'll be all, but if I were you, I'd watch your step. There's quite a few folks around here worried about you hanging around.'

'Oh?' Bushy eyebrows were raised quizzically. 'Why's that, Sergeant?'

'Because,' Hampson capped his ballpoint, returned it to his breast pocket, 'there's one helluva lot of nasty things been happening around here within the space of a week. Apart from the Deeps girl going missing, a village church has been razed to the ground, valuable parchments have been desecrated in the cathedral, the head verger collapsed and died of a heart attack on account of that, a couple were kicked and trampled to death by their horses, and a farmer accidentally baled himself in his baler. That's why you've attracted so much interest, Jonjo. *Folks are saying that you're a Jonah, that the disasters will go on until you've left the area.*'

'That almost sounds like a hint, Sergeant.'

'Take it how you like,' Hampson's expression was inscrutable, 'but I don't want to have to bring you in again. We'll be keeping an eye on you.'

'Oh, about that musician's licence, Sergeant?'

The policeman waved a dismissive hand. 'Off you go, Jonjo.'

'Thank you, Sergeant.' Jonjo rose to his feet, headed towards the door, closed it softly after him.

For some minutes the detective sat there staring at the emulsioned wall. The other had left him with a feeling of unease, not suspicion. He was satisfied in his own mind that Jonjo had not harmed Sharon Deeps, nor was he an arsonist or vandal. But his instinct was something that even a decade of CID work could not pinpoint. It went along with what the villagers were saying, that death and catastrophe would prevail until Jonjo was gone.

Hampson tried to calculate how long it was before they could expect the first frost.

Part Two
Autumn

CHAPTER FOURTEEN

Keith Richards had bought a tumbledown barn off Don Pocklington in 1985. He had spent a small fortune in converting it into what estate agents describe as a 'desirable residence', and his investment had resulted in a property worth in the region of a quarter of a million pounds within five years.

Keith was in his early fifties but a subtle dyeing of his greying hair had given him a somewhat younger, if not youthful, appearance. Tall and well built, he made his living out of postal bookselling, specializing in a few scarce and much sought after items, rather than filling his shelves with run-of-the-mill books. His hobby of gardening had maintained his fitness into middle age.

Mandy, his wife, was forty-five, and reasonably good-looking although she had succumbed to a weight problem in recent years. Somewhat fiery in temperament, she had found the move from a town house to a rural area somewhat dull and had chosen to continue her secretarial job in Lichfield on a part-time basis to alleviate her boredom. Her dislike of housework had resulted in Richard's agreeing to employ Bridget Chalmers as a domestic help.

Ten years younger than Mandy, Bridget was slim and attractive, with short fair hair and a vivacious personality. Since she had no transport of her own, it was necessary for Richard to fetch her from the neighbouring village around nine thirty on one morning a week, and take her home shortly after 3 p.m. in time to collect her nine-year-old daughter from school.

Bridget started her job at the Chapter House in early October and her zest for household chores was soon apparent. She and Richard had coffee together in the middle of the morning and a snack lunch around one. During these informal get-togethers, she confided in him, told him of her domestic problems which mostly cantered around her building worker husband, Ken. Ken was moody in the extreme, frequently resorted to childish tantrums during which he smashed crockery. She emphasized that he had never hit her but she lived in fear that he might. Keith sympathized with her, and found himself looking forward to that one day a week.

Thus it was a bitter disappointment to him when, in early December,

Bridget had to go into hospital for a minor operation. She would not be resuming her weekly job until the New Year. During Christmas week he drove over to her council house with a box of chocolates and a card from 'Keith and Mandy'. They drank tea and talked for an hour; Ken had been in one of his moods on the previous day and had broken one of the flimsy doors on the kitchen unit.

It was on Boxing Day night that Keith realized that he was in love with Bridget. It was an exciting thought, one that would probably go no further than pleasant fantasies but was strong enough to ruin his concentration during the main feature film on television which he and Mandy watched together. And when they retired to bed, it was Bridget to whom he made love, surprising his wife with an unexpected hour of fiery passion.

Of course, Bridget would never guess his feelings for her, but when she resumed her job in the second week of January she was suddenly the most important person in his life. He wanted to tell her of his love for her but his courage failed him. In all probability she would hand in her notice, perhaps fearing sexual harassment by a man seventeen years older then herself.

One Monday morning, a month later, Richard suddenly decided to tell her. An impromptu decision, his voice trembled a little, and she had no idea of what he was about to say.

'I. . . I've got something to tell you, Bridget.' He spilled some coffee in his saucer, stared down at the table.

'Go on then,' she laughed, 'or have I got to guess?'

'I missed you terribly whilst you were in hospital,' he confessed. 'In fact, I almost came to see you but I didn't know how your husband would react.'

'Oh, he wouldn't've minded. A lot of bosses visit their employees in hospital, don't they?'

'Then, over Christmas, I suddenly realized. . .'

'What, that nobody had done the hoovering and dusting?'

They both laughed, and then he blurted out, 'No, not that. I knew that I had fallen in love with you.'

She blushed, and looked away, muttered, 'I'm flattered.'

Their affair took until April to blossom although a relationship had developed between them. He didn't ask her out because he remembered that she had said she would never have an affair. Ken had once told her, 'If ever there's another bloke, I'll bloody kill you!' Keith was happy that he had confessed his love for her, and, in many ways, it was easier for both of them if it went no further. But there was a gradual escalation of their relationship and one day she told him in the car on the way home, 'Yes, I do have feelings for you but I'm not sure what they are.'

104

The next week Bridget seemed to have completed her routine housework by lunchtime. They lingered over a pizza lunch and when he suggested that they took their coffee through to the lounge, she nodded her agreement. They sat on the settee, his hand closed over hers and for the first time they kissed passionately.

The following week they made love in the spare bedroom. Her nervousness was only too apparent. 'Nobody but Ken and you have ever seen me naked.' Sex became a weekly routine, and then one day Richard suggested that they met somewhere during the week.

'I sometimes go for a walk up the wood on fine evenings when Ken's playing darts.' She was eager but hesitant. 'You could always be up there around eight thirty. There's never anybody else about.'

'All right.' His pulses raced. This was much more exciting than illicit passion in the comparative safety of the Chapter House. 'I'll leave the car down in the quarry and walk on up the track on Wednesday night.'

'I'll have to be home around ten.' She was nervous at the prospect. 'Ken usually gets back around half ten, occasionally before.'

That first time up in the wood had been more nerve-racking than on any of the previous occasions in the spare bedroom. The trees and undergrowth might have concealed a thousand watchers, and the couple started and peered into the gloom at every sound, the flapping of a pigeon, the rustling movements of a small rodent.

They were both secretly relieved when it was over and Bridget had hurried back to prepare Ken's supper and Keith was safe in his bookshelved refuge. After that they had reserved their illicit love for Monday afternoons in the house. Until early autumn.

'How about meeting up in the wood again?' Keith suggested. Almost five months had elapsed since that clandestine date, and those silly fears had become dim memories.

'I don't know.' Bridget's stock answer to anything she was uncertain about.

'Wednesday night?' At least she hadn't said no.

'That's my keep-fit night.'

'After keep-fit then?'

She pondered, played with her thumbs. 'All right then, but it'll be after nine. Ken's going away with the darts team; he won't be back till after eleven. But I'd better be home soon after ten.'

It was an unusually balmy night for early autumn. The weather still had not changed, and the only hint that summer was slipping away was a relenting of the burning daytime heat. The sun still shone out of cloudless skies, the countryside was browned and tinder dry, but the temperatures were bearable.

Keith was early; an eagerness for forbidden love saw him walking up the steep track ten minutes ahead of their scheduled time. He was nervous but he put it down to anticipation. Dusk was already creeping into the wood, the trees taking on weird gargantuan shapes, sinister giants that provided a canopy for him to walk under with their outstretched arms. Roosting birds fluttered uneasily. Something heavy crashed away through the undergrowth, probably a fox or a badger. He resisted the temptation to light a cigarette; Bridget did not approve of smoking. 'It's like kissing an empty ashtray,' she had told him one day, had then apologized in case she had caused offence.

She was late, seemed flustered when, much to his relief, she hurried into the clearing.

'I'm scared of the dark.' She had innumerable phobias. 'Keep-fit was late finishing. We mustn't be too long, though. It was creepy on the way up, there were things moving in the bushes. I hope there aren't any creepy-crawlies in the grass.'

'Most of them have died off or are hibernating by now.' He tried to sound reassuring.

'What about snakes?'

'They've long gone into their hideyholes for the winter.'

'I thought I heard some music playing somewhere on the way up.' She was tense, looking for excuses to cover up her feeling of guilt. 'Like. . . well, I can't explain it, sort of sad and eerie.'

'Sounds carry a long way on a still night,' which was why they were both subconsciously whispering. 'Maybe somebody has a radio playing loudly down in the village.' He listened intently but there was no sound to be heard. Everything had gone quiet; even the creatures of the wood were hushed. In a way it was sinister, as if they were waiting for something to happen.

They undressed, heaped their clothes in separate piles nearby. Keith spread his Barbour out on the ground; he had brought it for that specific purpose.

'I love you,' he whispered as they embraced.

She smiled in the gathering darkness.

'Do you love me?' Their affair had gone on for over six months now, and surely she would not have persevered with it if she didn't love him. She wasn't the kind of girl who just wanted extra-marital sex. Oh, please tell me that you love me.

'I've got feelings for you, like I said before.'

'How strong?'

'I don't know.' Then, 'What was that?'

He felt her stiffen, begin to tremble. 'I can't hear anything. . .' He could, a faraway sound that at first was like the buzzing of late evening insects, or a swarm of bees. Except that it was rhythmic, sad and lonely. The music which Bridget claimed to have heard earlier. 'It's somebody's radio. It's a long way off.'

'No, not that.' Her fingers gripped him, pinched his skin. 'Rustling movements. . . over there.' She pointed towards the dark, enshrouding forest.

'It's only rabbits.'

'Not rats? Or mice?'

'I doubt it. If they heard us, they'd run a mile.'

'I'm scared.' She clung to him. 'Let's go. Back to the car, anyway.' Wednesday dates were a disaster, he decided. Far better to stick to Mondays in the spare bedroom.

'All right, if it makes you feel any easier.'

She was reaching out for her discarded clothing when she screamed, a piercing shriek of terror that split the stillness.

'*Look!*'

He turned, saw something on the opposite side of the clearing, an indefinable shape approximately the size of a rabbit sitting up on its haunches. Then another. Further movements attracted his attention; there were half a dozen of them, maybe more. And Bridget began to scream again, hysterically.

He held her, tried to find an explanation, anything that would allay her fears. But he was scared, too, because they weren't rabbits or hares, the shape was wrong. Figures that stood upright, walked on two legs, had arms and a head. *Like miniature humans.*

Which was impossible. Until one of them stepped into a patch of grey dusk that filtered down through the canopy above and he glimpsed its rich, golden texture, saw its features, tiny eyes that glinted, mouth stretched into a malevolent grin.

'Oh, my God!' Bridget clung to him as he pulled her upright, somehow found the strength in his shaking limbs to lift her, carry her as he would have cradled a child.

Keith panicked, started to run, fleeing blindly back down the steep woodland track, his only thought to put as much distance between themselves and those creatures which had no right to exist on God's earth.

Only when nettles stung his bare thighs, briars tore at his flesh as though to impede him, did he remember their clothing lying back there in the clearing. He faltered, hesitated for one brief second, then ran on. No way was he going back. Whatever they were, they were in pursuit of the naked humans, Keith heard a rustling some yards behind, shrill piping sounds as though they called to one another. And somewhere, much closer than before, that music was playing. He recognized it as a mouth organ.

'Oh, Keith!' Bridget moaned her fear, began to sob.

'It's all right,' he was panting for breath, wondered how much further he could carry her, 'we're nearly back at the car now.' They weren't, there was a good hundred yards to go and he was limping where he had trodden on a sharp stone.

The little men were still coming, brushing through long grass and ferns, chattering incessantly as if they urged one another on. But they did not appear to have closed the gap, though he dared not pause to look back. Oh, Lord, what were they?

Thank God, the Escort was still where he had parked it, backed under a jutting outcrop in the old sandstone quarry, concealed from prying eyes. 'Here's the car.' He lowered Bridget to the ground, pulled her along with one hand, reached for the door handle with the other. Thank God he hadn't locked it, had left the keys in the ignition, a careless habit which he had developed from living out in the country. Hardly anybody in the village locked their vehicles.

She fell into the passenger seat, pulled the door shut. He heard the click of the lock as he raced round to the driver's side. Those creatures were spilling into the quarry, tiny shrieking figures heading for the parked vehicle.

He slammed his door, secured it. Bridget was sobbing, covering her eyes. He turned the ignition key, pumped the throttle with his bare foot. The engine whined, did not fire.

'Oh, no!' Sheer terror was stamped on her pallid features.

'It'll go,' he grunted, 'it never starts first time.'

It groaned, whined, died away. Something was pattering on the roof like the forerunners of a hailstorm, echoing tinnily in the interior. A movement on the bonnet startled him; something tapped on the windscreen. Bridget turned her head away, gave a stifled scream.

The tiny creatures were climbing all over the car: features the size of a ten pence coin squashed against the toughened glass, grinned their voyeuristic lust as they peered inside.

In that moment of mind-blowing terror, Keith recalled something Bridget had said to him the first time they made love. 'Nobody but Ken and you have ever seen me naked.' They had now.

At the third attempt the starter motor picked up, and he revved hard, desperate not to lose it. He flicked on the headlights, cringed from the scene they revealed. There were four of those things on the bonnet, closely woven figures of corn straw fashioned in the mocking image of man, horrific creatures that saw and understood as they jostled one another for a view of the naked woman in the passenger seat, squeaking lewdly, piping their obscenities, whilst in the background that strange music came hauntingly out of the autumnal darkness.

Bridget's thighs were pressed tightly together, her hands attempting to cover her breasts, her eyes closed.

'It's all right,' he tried to calm her fears, 'they can't get at us in here.' Can they?

He wondered for a moment if this was really happening, thought that he might be sleeping, that it was all just a nightmare. But it was real enough, and there were more of them up on the roof, another scratching on the rear window.

He let in the clutch and the car shot forward. The wheels bumped over the uneven ground and he tried not to see his unwelcome passengers on the bonnet. Their straw hands were scrabbling for a hold on the smooth glass, their feet slipping on the paintwork; screeching their anger, their faces contorted expressions of frustration. Then fear; it was their turn now.

Keith glided on to the tarmac lane, accelerated. A corn figure was gusted in the slipstream, whisked away like an autumn leaf in a gale. Then another. Those on the roof and at the rear followed in the wake of their companions. Only two remained, which in their cunning had secured a hold between the wipers and the windscreen.

'We'll soon fix you!' Keith laughed mirthlessly, pressed the wiper control. The blades swung upwards, took the creatures with them, a bizarre, miniature fairground ride with the passengers clinging on, squeaking their terror. Up, down, up again. Only one was left; its body beginning to flake in the wind, wisps of straw flying. Stubbornly, its legs gone, it refused to concede defeat; only half its grotesque body remained, those husk fingers tightening their grip, its features a malevolent mask that cursed him for what he was doing to it.

Just the head now, squashed flat between wiper blade and glass, a flattened corn straw skull whose features still lived and spat obscenities from the vile mouth, its moving lips squeaking harshly so that Bridget clasped her hands over her ears.

Finally, it was gone, too, a process of gradual destruction until just one last straw adhered to the rubber. Keith switched the wipers off, sighed his relief.

'Whatever were they?' Bridget still huddled in the embarrassment of nudity, cowered from the headlights of an oncoming car.

'I don't know.' His reply was shaky. 'Like living corn dollies. They've been saying in the village that there was something strange going on, I guess they were right.'

'They were horrible.'

'But they're gone, blown away to nothing.'

'There could be more of them.'

He did not reply. It was inconceivable that all those creatures had been destroyed in the Escort's slipstream.

'What are we going to do about our clothes?' She voiced her latest concern.

'Leave 'em where they are if we've got any sense.'

'But. . . but we have to go home. . .'

'With luck, that's no problem. It's dark, I'll back right up to your door and you can dash inside. It's too early for Ken to be home. As for me, Mandy's gone to one of those clothes parties and I'm not expecting her home till late.'

Wednesdays had never been lucky for them. From now on they had better keep to Mondays, nice and safe in the house. If anywhere was safe after what they had just experienced!

'I love you.' His hand found hers whilst he steered with the other one.

'I guess I love you, too, Keith,' she replied, and suddenly, for him, their trauma had been worth it, every terror-stricken second. The corn creatures had come but now they were gone. Nobody had been harmed. On this occasion it was only mischief.

CHAPTER FIFTEEN

The warmth of the Indian summer by day could no longer hold at bay the march of autumn. The leaves were turning a deep golden, the horse chestnuts already beginning to shed their foliage; the morning mists were thicker and took longer to disperse, wisping back over the countryside with the coming of dusk. The nights were chilly, and the first frosts were but a step away.

The Barkers, Don Pocklington and Johnson, the cathedral verger, were a month in their graves. Sharon Deeps had not been found, and her distraught parents still maintained a twenty-hour vigil beside the telephone; they had resigned themselves to the fact that their daughter was dead but the finding of her body would be a relief. They would not be able to rest until then. Canon Pilsbury had suffered a stroke and was hospitalized, his chances of a full recovery considered slender in view of his age. Avis Pocklington was bravely attempting to continue the running of the farm, assisted by Will at weekends. Neither of them had cried since the funeral, and then only as a token of a sham respect.

Jonjo's prophecy that Gubbins would return with the first frost would shortly be put to the test. The Kirbys had long since abandoned all hope of seeing her again. Perhaps the rebuilding of the village church would help to erase Ben's nightmarish memories.

Except that there was still an atmosphere of tension hanging over the farm and its surrounding land. The animals, both domestic and wild, were edgy as though they, too, sensed that the escalation of unknown evil had not yet reached its climax.

There was something out there that kidnapped and killed, a ruthless paranormal foe that singled out its victims with discerning malevolence, its motives unknown to all except itself. If its mark was on you, then you would not know until it was too late.

Dick Kirby shivered, told himself that his flesh goosepimpled because the nights were becoming chilly. Tomorrow he would put the sheep on the stubble, let them graze it for a week or so before he ploughed it in.

The sheep were reluctant to leave their parched pastureland in spite of the lack of grazing and their apparent fear of the place. Dick had opened

111

the gate leading into the stubble, let Patch, the family's ageing border Collie, range to and fro, attempting to herd the bleating animals. But somehow one always broke free, eluded the dog, and the rest followed. It was a never-ending circle of chaos. Now they were crowding the gateway where the Barkers had met their untimely end, rattling the gate, threatening to buckle it in their panic to break out into the roadway.

In the end he walked back to the yard and fetched the Land Rover. Driving into the meadow from the road brought back uncomfortable memories. Some nights he still heard the terrified screams of Tom and Rita as the shires reared at them, struck with their heavy hooves, rolled on their injured victims. But you had to put it out of your mind; life must go on.

Now Dick and Patch launched a two-pronged assault on the flock, channelled them towards the lower gate. They bunched in the open space, milled, as if some invisible barrier prevented them from going into the adjoining field.

He drew the vehicle sideways, stopped them from breaking back. Patch covered the narrow gap, snapped at them. Then, suddenly, as one they burst on to the stubble, huddled again, their plaintive bleats echoing in the still atmosphere. A mist was beginning to rise and it served to highlight the sheep's fear, silhouettes bunched together because there was safety in numbers, spectral shapes cringing before an unseen foe.

Dick walked through on to the stubble, latched the gate behind him. Patch would slip through the lower bars with ease, follow him. He wanted to ensure that there was enough weed growth in the barley stalks to sustain his livestock.

After ten yards he halted, aware that the sheepdog was not following. He turned, whistled. Patch was lying on the other side of the gate, watching his master with undisguised fear, tail curled under his body.

'Patch! Here, boy!'

There was no answering wag of the tail, no enthusiasm. The dog was cowed, as frightened as the sheep which he had helped to drive.

'All right, stay there, then!' Dick was annoyed, uneasy. He turned, walked away. There was an abundance of clover growing in the thick stubble; the sheep would be fine for a week, a fortnight at a pinch. During that time the autumn rains might come and the browned pastureland start to revive, provide enough grass for another month. By then the stubble would be turned in, and another cycle would begin.

He stopped suddenly, stared over the brow to where the land fell away gradually, thought that perhaps the evening mist had caused an optical illusion. Or maybe the long drought had scorched a discoloration on the stubble. Except that the circles, the shapes, were just too symmetrical to have been created by Nature herself. A prickling began at the base of his spine, travelled slowly upwards.

He stared with frightened amazement at the straight line of rings, perhaps a dozen or more of them, that stretched equidistant from one another down to the far hedgerow. Some were two or three yards in circumference, others barely eighteen inches; arrows jutted from them at varying degrees, two had triangles attached to their perimeters. From above they resembled a line of hieroglyphics etched in the stubble, the writings of an ancient scribe scratched on the ground, which the heatwave and its accompanying dryness had unearthed. Or, and he backed away at the very possibility, they were. . .

Crop circles.

Dick's mouth was dry. He glanced upwards, fearful lest some silent UFO might be hovering above, waiting to swoop, to snatch him and transport him to wherever Sharon Deeps and Gubbins had been taken. But the saffron sky was empty, not so much as a wisp of cirrus cloud in sight. His gaze travelled back to the weird markings, tried in vain to translate them into logic, sanity that was devoid of intrigue and terror.

He failed to come up with an explanation, recalled a centre spread feature article in one of the tabloids only last week, illustrated with photographs of markings which were identical to those in his own field. Over three hundred separate incidents had been reported on farmland in Oxfordshire and Wiltshire, their cause so far undiscovered, but rumoured to be signs from aliens who visited Earth under cover of darkness, left messages which were beyond our comprehension. *Perhaps prophesies of doom, trying to warn us before it was too late of some catastrophe which would destroy our planet.*

Rubbish, the kind of story designed to sell newspapers, theories that belonged to the science fiction magazines. His skin was prickling all over. There was no denying the fact that those same circles had appeared on his own land, were right here before his own eyes.

He clutched at proverbial straws; the markings down south had appeared in *growing* corn, as though ripening cereals held some attraction for the perpetrators; in which case he would surely have noticed them when he cut the barley, certainly when the sheaves were gathered. *Which meant that these had appeared since, within the last few days.*

He glanced nervously around him in the deepening dusk, saw imaginary visitors from another planet which turned out to be his own sheep, the animals clustered on the brow, afraid to venture down to where the strange markings lay. As though they knew. . .

And back at the meadow gate Patch was whining, beginning to howl mournfully. There was an old country saying that when a dog howled somebody was about to die. . .

Dick backed way, scattered the sheep but they did not go far, bunched again and bleated. In the morning he would return, examine the circles more closely. For the moment he would say nothing to Brenda, but if they were still there tomorrow then perhaps he could turn them to his advantage. A word to the press would mean a fresh influx of paying visitors. . .

'It's all right, Patch.' he found himself whispering, saw that the collie had retreated from the gate, was standing by the Land Rover, staring back towards the meadow. There was a low warning growl in the dog's throat, and that was when Dick noticed the shadowy figure leaning up against the gatepost on the roadside.

Jonjo! Dick thought that the busker had left the district. He had neither seen nor heard of him for a week at least. Damn the fellow, still hanging around; Dick had a good mind to phone the police. He climbed up into the Land Rover, Patch jumping over the tailboard, swung round and drove in the direction of the roadside gate. The headlights picked Jonjo out, and as Dick drew up alongside he saw how he had changed.

Jonjo's cheeks were sunken, hollowed, and he had an almost cadaverous look about him. His shoulders were hunched, bowed, as if he was troubled by a bout of arthritis; his beard was flecked with grey, a sudden process of ageing that made it less difficult to guess his years. It was as though the colder nights had begun to wither him like a tender plant when the summer warmth waned. In spite of everything that had gone before, you found yourself pitying him.

Dick slowed to a standstill. He killed the engine but left the lights on, just as he would have done to speak to a neighbour whom he had not seen for a week or two. It would have been churlish to have driven past, ignored him.

Patch was pressed up in the furthermost corner, still growling; Dick heard the dog trembling, maybe getting ready to howl again.

'Hi, Jonjo!' It was the first time that he had greeted the other amicably, sensed a comfort in his presence after what he had seen. The police had interviewed the wandering musician and they had okayed him, seemed satisfied. Unless, of course, it was another case of lack of evidence. 'What brings you here?'

'The same as you, Mr Kirby,' Jonjo's voice was rasping, hinting at ageing lungs and a cracking voicebox. 'I have been to look at the circles. I guessed they might show up round here soon.'

'Why's that?' Had the busker marked them himself, possibly as a distraction to divert suspicion from himself? 'You've been trespassing on my land again.' Trying to appear angry but it was an act that fell short. The figure standing in the glare of the headlights was no longer sinister,

114

just pathetic. Maybe he was ill, had caught pneumonia and was stubbornly refusing to see a doctor, believing that his cure lay in Nature's own remedies, natural medicines from the fields and hedgerows.

'Because after all that has happened there had to be a final warning.'

'From whom?'

'Nature.' Jonjo still leaned on the post. Dick thought that without its support the other might have fallen. But though the body had weakened perceptibly, those dark eyes were as keen as ever. 'She has tolerated man's abuse for too long. Finally she has to do something about it.'

'Like taking my goat?'

'Perhaps.' Jonjo toyed with his harmonica, 'I only know what I see. But her warning is written clearly on your field.'

'You understand those circles?' Dick's eyes narrowed, suspicious again.

'Only in their broadest terms. Suffice to say they are a final warning. Unless those who are responsible for tending the land relent in their constant abuse of it, the consequences will be too terrible to contemplate.'

Dick nodded. Whether or not Jonjo had made those marks, there was no denying the threat to the environment which farmers such as Don Pocklington had created; chemicals destroyed insect and plant life that was vital to the survival of many species. That was why the partridge and many songbirds that were common years ago had declined, some to the verge of extinction. Slurry spills into rivers wiped out fish populations; the felling of trees destroyed a source of the oxygen which was vital to life itself. For years mankind had been hell-bent on a course of self-destruction.

'What can I do?' There was a note of despair in Dick Kirby's voice.

'You are doing everything that could possibly be asked of you.' Jonjo eased himself away from the post, swayed unsteadily. 'In a very small way you are helping to put things right, but it has to be done on a worldwide scale. You are teaching people how to take a harvest and put something back, how to treat the environment which gives you life with respect. You feed the soil so that it will feed you the following season. You cull, but you leave sufficient to reproduce. So it should be everywhere, but in recent years man has taken without giving back. His greed will be his downfall, his destruction. You, my friend, are teaching others your ways, which is why there is still hope.'

'Who are you, Jonjo?'

'Just. . . Jonjo the busker. I only know what I see and hear, try to pass the word on to others.'

'That music you play. . .' Dick hoped that the other would not play his instrument again. Even now, the strains returned to plague him from

115

time to time, sometimes in his sleep.

'Music is so relaxing.' The busker stroked his harmonica lovingly. 'It calms, soothes. Animals like it, too. It helps at a time like this, you see. They know more than we do, and they are very disturbed.'

'So I've noticed, Jonjo.' Dick sighed, 'I don't know who you are or what you're doing here, but I hear what folks are saying. They're scared of you. So am I, because of what might happen to my family.'

'*You* have no need to fear, Mr Kirby,' Jonjo's expression was one of hurt, 'you and your family are safe because you are doing the right things.'

'Maybe, but whatever it is that's kidnapping and killing in this locality has taken my goat. How do I know that next time it won't be my wife or my son?'

'It won't, I assure you. Perhaps your goat was a mistake, I cannot say. But I am certain she will be returned when the frost comes. Perhaps they had need of her, just borrowed her.'

'*They?*'

'Nature's servants. Her army, if you like.'

'Those who set fire to the church, destroyed the Gospels in the cathedral, caused the Barkers' horses to turn on them?'

'Yes, but do not blame them. They were provoked. Many of the animals are rebelling, too. They sense a revolution that is simmering to the boil. Others are just nervous, frightened. Mr Kirby, there is nothing I can do to halt it now, it has gone too far. Only mankind's willingness to change will save him. Perhaps the frosts will provide a breathing space for him to get his act together, or at least to show his repentance. I don't know; it is not up to me.'

'What are these corn creatures?' Dick watched the other carefully; Jonjo was leaning back against the gatepost again.

'As I said, they are Nature's own. Show them respect and they are the guardians of the crops, symbols of fertility itself. Abuse them and they will fight for what is rightfully theirs. In the latter case, their wrath is terrible to behold. I can do nothing to influence or control them, I assure you of that, Mr Kirby. *At the moment, everything has escalated out of control.*'

'Thank you, Jonjo.' Dick felt suddenly tired to the point of exhaustion. He was confused. Perhaps it would have been better not to have asked for even now he did not understand.

'One thing, though. If I am doing the right things, why have they left their final warning on my land?'

'Because they are looking to you to warn others, Mr Kirby.'

Which was why Jonjo had deliberately waited by the gate for him, Dick concluded. His voice was slightly husky when he spoke again. 'Look,

Jonjo, the nights are becoming colder. If you want to sleep in my hay barn, you're welcome.'

'I thank you, Mr Kirby, but I never sleep under a roof. My place is beneath the hedgerows; I am part of the environment which I am trying to protect.'

Dick parked the Land Rover in the yard, stood there listening to the unbroken quiet of an autumn night. No owl hooted in the big wood, the sheep were no longer bleating up on the stubble field. Even Patch had stopped whimpering, lying cowed in the back of the vehicle.

It was the stillness which frightened Dick most because he was afraid of what might happen when it was broken. He trembled as he recalled the recent violent deaths: Pocklington and the Barkers, the verger in the cathedral, and Sharon Deeps who was missing out there somewhere. And the perpetrators had delivered their final ultimatum which was impossible to meet. There would be more deaths, and he prayed that Jonjo's assurance was not simply idle words and Brenda and Ben would be safe.

CHAPTER SIXTEEN

'I think it's wrong to burn the stubble, Mum.' Will Pocklington had scarcely spoken throughout tea, had obviously been deep in thought.

'I agree with you.' Avis was relieved that he had confided his worry in her, for she had wondered what was troubling him. Will had changed noticeably since his father's death. Gone were those fits of uncontrollable temper, the arrogance with them. The boy was obviously thinking deeply; even at his age he realized that he had been influenced by his father. It would be a good job when school started again.

'Couldn't we bale the straw and sell it?' he asked at length.

'It would cost too much. Your father used to say the twine cost more than he would get for the straw itself. Until the solicitor has settled everything up and we know just what we're going to do, we'll have to carry on as before. In the meantime, Mr Mack will help us out with the ploughing and the harvesting and we'll have to be guided by what he says.'

'I don't like Mr Mack, Mum.'

'I can't say I'm awfully struck on him either,' Avis replied tactfully. Most of the farmers did not care much for Johnny Mack but few could do without him throughout the year. Tall and slightly overweight, Johnny Mack, the agricultural contractor, was seldom seen without a pair of oily overalls, a growth of beard stubble and thick unwashed hair. Renowned for his continual obscene language, he had a violent temper, and it was rumoured that he beat his long-suffering wife. At forty-two, he had spent most of his life on the seat of a tractor, either hedge-cutting, ploughing and sowing, or harvesting for those farmers who needed assistance. Whatever his shortcomings, his work was exemplary; none could fault him, so they hired him year after year. It was with some reluctance that Avis had telephoned him two days after Don's funeral; there was no way that she was going to be able to run the farm without hired labour. Don had refused to pay wages, even for casual seasonal work, and she wondered how Johnny Mack would react.

'I dare say I could help you, Mrs Pocklington.' His tone was gruff. 'I'll 'ave to fit it in considering your problems. I suppose you want me to finish the 'arvest for you?'

'No, no, the corn's all in, it's just a question of ploughing in the stubble.'

'The straw'll 'ave to be burned first.' There was almost a belligerence about the way he spoke. 'I'll see to it one night next week. Then I'll come up and plough the fields for you.'

Avis had no option other than to go along with the straw-burning idea. She consoled herself with the thought that Don would have burned it, anyway, so it wouldn't be any different. Perhaps next year, when she had got the farm organized, she would work it differently. If it had not been for Will she would have sold up, but her son showed an enthusiasm for farming so she had to keep the land until he was ready. Maybe she would let it out for grazing next year, just let it tick over and earn its keep until Will left school. But, in the meantime, she would leave it up to Johnny Mack. She could not afford to offend him.

'I think I'll have a walk up to the big field.' Will got up from the table.

'Why?' She tensed. Don had been killed in the field next to the big one, and neither herself nor Will had been up there since.

'Just to look.'

'It'll be dark in an hour, Will.'

'I'll be back by then, Mum.'

'Oh, all right.' Maybe the boy felt that he needed to start getting about the farm again. 'But mind that you are back by dark.' Because they haven't found the Deeps girl yet and we don't know who's prowling about.

Will experienced a sadness as he left the farmhouse, resisted the urge to cry. Not because his father was dead – that was all in the past once the funeral was over. Rather it was because of what his father had been; not just his rages but the way he had deliberately set out to antagonize and oppose everything and everybody. Don Pocklington had delighted in grubbing out established hedgerows and felling mature trees; not surreptitiously as many farmers did, but ensuring that others were aware of his sadistic intentions, defying preservation orders and then paying the paltry fines with smug satisfaction because the damage was already done. Once he had submitted plans for a row of houses on the field adjoining the road, knew full well that they would be turned down. But his motive was to outrage the villagers, the newcomers, the 'outsiders' as he referred to them. He had succeeded.

Most of all, though, Don Pocklington enjoyed stubble-burning time. He talked about it long before the harvest was ready; indeed, Avis thought that the crop of straw was worth more to him than the grain yield, sadistic pleasure before money. He wanted the wind 'just right', blowing from the fields straight down to the village. Usually, he waited for dusk because night time was when he could cause the maximum aggravation; most people slept with a bedroom window open. Last autumn both Avis

119

and Will had feared for his sanity as he sat at the kitchen table rattling a box of matches, savouring the moment when he would touch the dry straw with a tiny brimstone flame. Within seconds that flame would grow to a roaring inferno, sweeping diagonally across the stubble, fanned by a stiff breeze. The night sky would turn yellow and orange, the racing clouds taking on fearsome hues, dragons roaring across the heavens.

A smoke pall reminiscent of a miniature Hiroshima had hung over the village that night. The atmosphere had been hot and suffocating, smuts floating down like a black snowstorm, lying on roofs and lawns, soiling washing that had been inadvertently left out. The line of flames had got out of control; the inadequate ploughed area of firebreak had no chance of stopping the inferno. The thick roadside hawthorn hedge was like kindling; a spectacular column of shooting sparks, a living, blazing skeleton of some elongated prehistoric beast roaring with pain and rage, the fire spilling on to the verge. A concerted effort by two fire crews saved the nearest house, but they had to spend the following day damping down the sizzling, smoking grass to be sure that the flames were extinguished.

Don was fined £100, and for him it was money well spent. Entertainment value. Next year, he had vowed, it would be on an even grander scale; he had increased his acreage of grain, there would be double the quantity of straw to burn. He would fire as fast as he could drive the pickup from one torching point to the next.

Which, Will reflected, was yet another good reason for Don Pocklington's death. But it wouldn't make any difference to the stubble-burning, Johnny Mack would see to that. Maybe the contractor wasn't vindictive towards the villagers; he simply did not care. He was paid to burn stubble and the more he incinerated the bigger his cheque at the end of the month. When he left hedge-trimmings littering the lanes during the winter months, he was not deliberately bent on puncturing the tyres of passing motorists, it was all a question of how many miles of hedges his flail-cutter could cover in a day. Clearing up the cuttings was a non-profit-making exercise. People complained, but by the time the police called and requested him to sweep the roads, the winds had done it for him. Nobody was going to go to the trouble to prosecute him under some obscure section of the Highways Act.

Will knew that it was going to be a repeat performance of last autumn, the sky a smoky red, the village obscured by thick, opaque smoke. The telephone would ring and ring, until finally his mother took it off the hook. Then the police would come, but not even the most officious officer could expect a farmer's widow to put out fifty acres of burning stubble. Will had overheard his mother requesting Mr Mack over the phone to take care with the fire; she had listened unconvinced to his assurances.

When it came to the night in question all he would be interested in was as many acres of straw ash as possible on which to base his charges.

Will stood in the open gateway staring across the stubble plain. Only a few years ago this same area had comprised seven separate fields. His father had bulldozed out the hedgerows, regardless of scenic beauty and wildlife habitat. The fewer hedges to shade the growing crop the better. Daylight and sunlight were calculated in money as far as Don Pocklington was concerned. If songbirds and partridges suffered as a result, then that meant fewer beaks to peck the ears of corn.

A mist was rolling in with the dusk, wispy streaks of grey like forerunners of the smoke that would eddy across these same fields tomorrow when Johnny Mack ignited the straw. The boy felt guilty, wished he could apologize to the landscape for what his father had done to it and what the contractor was about to do. He wondered if there was any way of preventing the latter from carrying out such an outrage, but if his mother had done her best to moderate it, a young boy was powerless to intervene.

He stood with bowed head, promised himself that when he inherited the farm things would be different. Tomorrow he would go round to the Kirbys', say sorry to Ben for those jibes. Maybe they could be mates again, farm side by side one day.

Will decided that he had better go home. Dusk was merging into darkness and the night was cold. Soon they could expect the first frost, if not tonight then tomorrow.

He had already turned to walk away when he heard the music. At first he thought it might have been the humming of a cloud of midges mourning the departure of the balmy nights. No, there was a rhythm to it, he sensed its sadness, like the way the organ had played when they followed his father's coffin out of church. Except that on that occasion Will was not really sad.

He wanted to go home but for some reason he could not. His feet moved but he had no control over them, was unable to prevent them from turning, felt the stubble cracking and crunching beneath his soles.

Walking on, the mist parting before him, closing back in behind him. All around him the straw rustled as though he disturbed small rodents, sent them scurrying away.

The music was louder now, seemed to be calling him through the mist, a summons which he was powerless to ignore. Whoever it was, he would tell them that he was sorry for what his father had done and one day he would do his best to put things right. In the meantime, they would have to put up with Mr Mack burning the stubble.

121

'The telephone's ringing!' Brenda Kirby stirred, dug her elbow into Dick's side, heard him grunt. 'Dick, the phone!'

'All right,' he took a few seconds to struggle out of a deep sleep. He glanced at the digital alarm clock on the bedside table, its luminous dial ticking away the seconds with ruthless regularity. 3.08.

'You'd better answer it, Dick.'

He said 'All right' again, a combination of annoyance at being disturbed and fear of bad tidings. Calls at this time were seldom good news.

She heard him padding across the bedroom, the click of the door handle, then a shaft of landing light slanted in through the door. Her heart was pounding; she made as if to throw the bedclothes back and follow her husband, but she didn't. Her instinct was to pull the sheets up over her and clap her hands over her ears so that she would not be tempted to eavesdrop. The phone had stopped ringing; she could hear Dick talking but could not make out the words.

Now he was coming back upstairs, fast footsteps that heralded bad news. I don't want to hear.

The bright light dazzled her but not enough to hide her husband's expression, the shock stamped on his white features.

'Will's missing now!' he said.

'Oh, my God! Ben. . .'

'I've just checked on him. He's okay.'

'Thank God!' Sheer relief, so selfish. A sole survivor from a shipwreck and you prayed that it was your own kin. You prayed that everybody else had drowned and yours had been spared.

'That was the police.' He sat on the side of the bed and she saw how he shook. 'They're going to launch a full-scale search at daybreak. I'm going with them.'

Brenda nodded. They wouldn't find Will Pocklington, any more than they had found Sharon Deeps or Gubbins. It seemed that you just walked away and were never seen again. Tomorrow she would keep Ben indoors.

Dick sat there, not talking. He recalled how he had met Jonjo by the roadside gate. He hadn't told the police, he wouldn't unless they asked. Because he believed the busker when he had told him that he had no control over events. And, anyway, Jonjo was ill, that much had been apparent.

'Oh, Dick,' there was near-hysteria in Brenda's voice, 'how much longer is this going on? I can't stand any more!'

'I think it's nearly over.' His hand found hers, squeezed it reassuringly.

He crossed to the window, drew back the curtains and looked out. The night was chilly but not cold enough for a frost. Maybe tomorrow night.

CHAPTER SEVENTEEN

Johnny Mack had been working at the Sheets' farm most of the day. Clive Sheet had baled his straw because he needed it for his small herd of cattle. He had not had time to carry the bales and with the weather experts forecasting a change, he had called in the contractor.

It was not often that Johnny under-estimated a job, but this time he had planned on finishing by six and it was after seven by the time he drove the last trailer load into the farmyard. It didn't really matter, though, because he could set fire to the Pocklingtons' stubble any time. He would do it on his way home, and bugger staying there to keep an eye on it. It would be all right. He had ploughed the firebreaks the other day. Nobody would bother, they were all too busy searching for the missing boy. Will Pocklington was the least of Mack's worries. Kids ran away from home every day, they either turned up or they didn't.

Johnny Mack drove a four-wheel-drive Chevrolet, similar in appearance to a Range Rover but, in his own estimation, more macho. There was a dent on the wing where he had hit an Escort on one of the bends in the narrow lanes; the driver of the written-off vehicle had reported him to the police for dangerous driving but there were no witnesses, and the insurance companies had agreed on a knock-for-knock payout. Mack preferred to leave his own damage on show, a kind of warning to other road users of what to expect if they clashed with him.

It was dusk by the time he arrived at the Pocklingtons' farm. He avoided the farmyard, drove straight on up to the fields. He had no wish to be delayed by accounts of how young Will had disappeared, or questioned by the police. Time was money. He accelerated, left a cloud of dust in his wake.

The weather was certainly on the change. No rain in the offing – the gathering mist was a guarantee of another sunny day tomorrow – but the cold had an intensity about it that heralded frost. It would freeze tonight for the first time since the summer, just enough to nip any tender plants.

He parked on the corner of the big field, surveyed the expanse of golden stubble that went on and on, dipped beyond the skyline. He wouldn't even need a splash of petrol; the straw was dry enough. He needed to ignite six places in order to create a line of fire that would sweep downwards, burn the whole area. Box of matches in hand, he climbed out of the vehicle. The dusk was already turning to darkness; he could only just make out the hedgerows.

Something rustled the loose straw ahead of him. It was probably a covey of partridges jukking down for the night. Well, they had two choices, he laughed to himself: take off somewhere else or end up roasted. He didn't care which.

He would walk to the furthest point, start his fires from there, be back in the Chevy before the inferno took hold. In any case, the wind would sweep the flames away from him; there was no danger.

There seemed to be a lot of partridges in the straw tonight. He could hear them moving about, uneasy because a human was in close proximity. The drop in temperature was the reason; the straw was beautifully warm. But not half as warm as it would be in a few minutes. He laughed again.

There, that should do. He began scraping some of the straw into a pile with his foot, eased a match out of the box. Jeez, what was *that*!

A kind of shrill squeal had him peering about him, a screech that embodied anger and hate. Whatever it was, it was too dark to see it now. Probably a stoat or some other carnivorous animal, he decided. Well, whatever it was, it would soon be fleeing for its life. Mack struck a match, dropped it into the pile of straw. For a moment he thought that the flame had gone out, then it was crackling, sending up a column of smoke. An orange tongue of fire began to devour the dry stalks, already spreading out to catch the rest of the straw.

He hastened to retrace his steps, stopping to fire another pile. OK, there was no danger, but fire was frightening. A good servant but a bad master and you were always afraid of it taking over, no matter how many precautions you had taken. Three fires now, the first one running and leaping, a wall of flames three feet high rushing to join up with the adjacent pyre. He lit the fourth.

And that was when it seemed that the whole field was screaming its wrath at him.

Johnny Mack dropped the matchbox, had to scrabble on the ground until he found it. Damn, the matches had all tipped out, spilled down into the straw. His trembling fingers searched for them but it would be impossible to find them without a torch. There was a lamp in the truck; he'd better go back for it and. . .

The screeching was ear-splitting, mind-numbing. Johnny Mack staggered back, cried out at the pain inside his head. *Then he screamed hysterically because it was as if the entire field had come to life, tiny silhouettes that ran and danced. An angry horde gleaming orange and golden in the light from the spreading fire.*

They were everywhere, ragged miniature effigies, demons that shrieked their fury at this human who had dared to set fire to their domain. They surrounded him, tiny warriors of the wild, pointing, gesticulating. Johnny tried to flee but his feet refused to move, like one of those nightmares where you tried to run but your limbs would not respond to your brain.

Now their cries were drowned by the crackling of the flames; the heat fanned his body, dried his sweat, began to scorch him. *The fire which should have gone on downhill with the night breeze had changed course, was racing towards him with the speed of a running man.*

Even at the height of his terror he was aware that those creatures, whatever they were, had gone. If they had stayed they would have burned, shrivelled up, browned with the intense heat, just as the stubble around him was parching. A cloud of smoke enveloped him, had him retching, trying to breathe, blinded as his eyes streamed. Again he tried to move but it was as though his feet were embedded in concrete, his arms paralysed by a stroke.

There was music playing somewhere which was stupid, it was all in his fear-crazed mind. A loud explosion shook the ground beneath him; he was aware of a vivid flash to his left. He knew that it was the Chevrolet that had exploded.

Even screaming was denied him. He opened his mouth, tried to force a cry of terror, but only his lips moved round his parched tongue. Trapped in a fiery hell, he writhed as his oily overalls began to smoulder, his body dehydrating, the flesh expanding on his bones like taut, ancient vellum. Burning as he stood upright, a Guy Fawkes effigy without a supporting stake, his skin shrivelling, starting to melt. He prayed for death but it mocked him right until the very end, the line of fire sweeping round in defiance of the direction of the wind, a horseshoe inferno that turned back on itself, then halted momentarily before picking up its intended route and rushing on downwards towards the village, gathering momentum as it fanned out, driving those tiny, ragged figures before it.

Mandy Richards craved a cigarette, was tempted to help herself to one out of the ivory box on top of the cocktail cabinet. Had it been within reach she would have undoubtedly yielded to temptation even though she had not smoked for almost a year now. Because there were occasions when tobacco was all that was left to turn to, and this was one of those occasions.

Her hands trembled as she wrung them together, her features were strained, shock had stamped its mark upon her. She glanced at the other three in turn, waited for somebody to say something. Nobody spoke.

125

They were all looking to her, putting the ball in her court.

Keith was possibly the most composed of all, biting on the nylon stem of his pipe, tense. Bridget was crying, dabbing at her eyes with a screwed-up tissue, trembling, glancing nervously at her husband who had adopted a posture of defiance, standing with his back to the mantelpiece, seemingly oblivious of the marks which his working boots had left on the lounge carpet. Mandy thought that had this meeting been in the living room of his own council house, he might well have become violent. Towards Keith and Bridget, anyway.

'I. . . I'm devastated.' Mandy broke the awkward silence, began tracing the pattern on the new carpet with her eyes. 'I can't believe it!'

'Well, you'd better start to.' Ken's jaw jutted as he stabbed a forefinger in the direction of his wife. 'I've told 'er, over the years, that if ever there was another bloke, I'd bloody kill 'er. But 'e's welcome to 'er,' pointing at Keith now, 'the bloody pair deserve each other. 'Er stuff's all in the porch, except what's in the fitted wardrobe, 'er best clothes. I'm sellin' them. The house is in my name and I'm not 'avin' 'er back inside it, 'cause I'd kill 'er for sure, then!'

Keith cleared his throat, made as if to say something but changed his mind. An affair that might well have gone on for years had been exposed by Ken Chalmers' sheer animal-like cunning. Last Monday, when he took Bridget home, they had gone into the house; you always knew if Ken was home because he parked his old banger outside the garage block opposite. His own garage was crammed full of junk.

There was no sign of the car so they presumed that the house was empty. Little did they guess that Bridget's husband was lying on the bed upstairs, the bedroom door ajar so that he could hear everything that was said down below. His eavesdropping had confirmed his suspicions that his wife and her Monday employer were having an affair. Ken's car was parked out of sight on the top end of the estate. True to his cunning nature, he had not revealed his findings until tonight when he was in a particularly bad mood, having lost at darts. On his return home he had confronted his wife, dragged her into the car and driven straight to the Chapter House. Keith had the impression that secretly the other was enjoying this and wanted to cause the maximum amount of trouble possible. Which he certainly had done.

'Well, Keith,' Mandy's voice trembled, 'I want to know what you're going to do!'

''E can do what 'e bloody likes,' Ken Chalmers interrupted, pulling open the door, 'and so can that cow!' A grubby hand was pointed in Bridget's direction. 'It makes no difference to me what they do, 'cause 'er ain't comin' back to my 'ouse. It's in my name. 'Er can run and get 'er stuff out o' the porch and 'ope I doesn't catch 'er! You can all please yer bloody selves!'

It was at that instant that Mandy smelled smoke and for a second everything else was forgotten. She heard Ken slam the front door after him. A whiff of burning made her cough and then smoke was seeping into the room trickling in through the partly open window behind the closed curtains. She rushed forward, pulled them apart, gave a cry at the scene which confronted her.

It seemed as if the entire sloping field that bordered their garden was on fire, the night sky a sinister smoky orange colour. The hawthorn hedge, which was the extremity of their garden, was blazing, the tongues of flame already licking at the wooden tool shed.

The other two crowded her, stared in disbelief and horror. Bridget screamed, not because of the inferno but because of the brief glimpse which she was afforded in its sinister light of a tiny figure fleeing from the flames. She felt her legs going weak beneath her, held on to Keith and hoped that he would stand by her. For surely those terrifying creatures who had discovered their infidelity in the wood that night had brought not only Ken but the fires of hell upon the adulterous couple, had punished them with their own brand of moral justice.

She was poised for a second scream when unconsciousness claimed her and she slumped against the woman she had wronged. Outside, the flames had leaped the lawn, were crackling the dry boughs of the shrubbery, an inferno of retribution roaring towards the house.

CHAPTER EIGHTEEN

Avis Pocklington stood at the bedroom window and watched the wall of fire sweeping down the stubble field, heading towards the house. She gave way to yet another spasm of coughing; the smoke was seeping into the house even though all the windows were closed. Her throat was sore, her eyes streamed, but she made no move to leave.

She blamed Don because he would have torched the straw in just the same way. Johnny Mack had only done what he had been asked to do, but burning a small stubble field was obviously one thing, a twenty acre plain quite another. Once the flames took hold they were unstoppable; firebreaks were merely a token safety precaution to comply with the Ministry's guidelines.

She heard fire engines speeding into the village; the community's safety was paramount. Maybe they would evacuate the fringe houses. The Chapter House, where that bookseller lived, was in the firing line, would probably be the first to go.

The farm didn't stand a chance; she was glad that all the livestock were out of doors. Then the farmhouse; she was glad in a way, had made up her mind to go with it. If Will had been here then they would have fled. But he wasn't, he was dead, just as the Deeps girl was. Once kids went missing, you gave up hope these days. She wanted to die and this was the best way, in her own home. There was nothing left to live for.

She heard the kitchen door slam shut. It was probably the wind. Footsteps; she tensed, listened. There was definitely somebody in the house, walking about down below. Sudden hope. She dared not even think that it might be Will but she had to know for sure. Trembling, her footsteps uncertain, she groped her way out of the bedroom across to the top of the stairs.

Somebody knocked against the kitchen table, rattled the dirty crockery which she had not bothered to clear away. She was almost afraid to call out, and when finally she did it was in a croaky whisper, unrecognizable as her own voice.

'Will. . . Will, is that you?'

'Avis!' An answering call that was tinged with relief. The voice was familiar and yet she was unable to place it, only knew that it was not her missing son's.

128

'Avis, what the hell are you doing stopping here?' Footsteps hurried towards the stairs, began to mount them. A figure came into view, coughing in the smoke. It was Dick Kirby. Avis held on to the stair rail, her slight hope dashed; she had not really believed it, anyway.

'I'm all right, Dick.'

'No, you're not.' There was concern on his bearded features. 'Thank God I found you. You've got to get out of here. The fire's out of control and there's every chance that this place will go up. There's relief fire crews on their way from Burton and Sutton but I doubt they'll be in time.'

'I'd prefer to stay, thank you.'

'Don't be stupid.' His strong fingers grasped her wrist, began to lead her down to the hall. 'There's no point in dying unnecessarily.'

'I want to.'

'What about Will?'

'He's dead, I know it.'

'He hasn't been found, and until they find him dead, there's always hope. The same goes for Sharon Deeps. My own hunch is that they'll both turn up.'

For some illogical reason she believed him and allowed herself to be led outside to where the Land Rover stood with its engine idling.

Daylight came, a thick, choking smoky grey that blended with the mist that had formed during the early hours. Brenda was indoors attempting to comfort Avis, Ben was asleep in his room; the novelty of a full-scale fire-fighting operation had finally exhausted him.

Dick went back outside, aware for the first time that there was a frost, much more severe than usual for the time of year. A rime was visible through the murky gloom, glinting on the slate roofs of the outbuildings; a puddle cracked beneath his wellington boots. He shivered, and not just because of the cold.

God, he was tired. Five fire crews had been called in to fight the blaze; three had been fully employed attempting to prevent the inferno spreading into the village itself. The Chapter House, like Pocklington's farm, was a gutted, smoking ruin. Fortunately, there had been no casualties, just a phenomenal insurance bill to be sorted out afterwards.

In the distance he heard the siren of yet another fire engine. And then the clanking of the cattle-grid beyond the yard. Somebody was coming, maybe a fireman to check that everything was all right this end. Or the doctor to look at Avis. Brenda had surreptitiously phoned Dr Gorman at home. Avis might need sedating, not because of the fire but because the reality of Will's disappearance had finally sunk in. He was gone, and she would never see him again. Even Dick's optimism had waned. You couldn't rely on the prophecy of a wandering musician no matter how strong your hunch was.

A red Sierra swung into the yard, its tyres crackling through the puddle where the farm water supply overflowed even in a drought. A young fair-haired man got out, an envelope clutched in his hand.

Christ, if he's a rep, at this hour and at a time like this. . . Dick's aggression showed in his expression, but the other nodded, smiling.

'I'm sorry to bother you, Mr Kirby,' A hand was proffered which Dick clasped limply. 'My name's Tim Weale.' A card was produced, a London address, a features reporter on one of the tabloids. 'I'd like to show you something.'

'I really don't have time to. . .' Dick's words tailed off as he glimpsed a blown-up aerial photograph of his own farm, the focal point the barley stubble, those weird markings emphasized by some modern photographic processing.

'You recognise it?'

'Yes, it's my farm.' Dick tensed. 'Who. . .'

'This was taken yesterday afternoon by a photographer working for a firm specializing in aerial photographs. He noticed the markings, developed his film right away and phoned our office. Looking for a quick buck, of course.' The reporter laughed. 'All the same, it does tie in with similar corn circles which we ran a feature on earlier in the summer. Those were in Oxfordshire and Wiltshire. There have never been any found further north. I take it you don't know about them?'

'I never even guessed,' Dick lied. The last thing they needed right now was reporters swarming all over the farm.

'I'd like to take a closer look at them, Mr Kirby.'

'All right.' If he refused then this guy would sneak up there, anyway. 'Though it's hardly the best of mornings for viewing corn circles.'

'You just show me, Mr Kirby, and I'll wait until this smoke and mist clears. Of course, there'll be a cheque coming your way. Maybe we could work a story out between us. You know – "Circles discovered after huge stubble fire" – make it really dramatic.'

Dick did not reply, walked on ahead. The atmosphere was heavy with the acrid stench of burning, and smoke was still eddying from Pocklington's fields. Dick coughed. He was lucky. All he had to worry about was the stink.

'This is the field.' He led the other towards the visitors' viewing point; even in this murk they should be able to make out the strange markings from there. Then he would leave the reporter to write his story. There was much to be done today.

'Now, if you look down here, according to that photograph, the circles

130

should be. . .'

Dick Kirby stared in astonishment, gripped the post and rail fence. Visibility was clearer up here, you could see almost as far as the opposite hedgerow. Just stubble with clover sprouting through it, the sheep grazing peacefully. But there was not a circle to be seen, not so much as a hint of where they had been yesterday.

'I. . .' Tim Weale stared in astonishment, 'there's no circles here. You must've mistaken the field.'

'Check it with your photo if you don't believe me.' Dick was trembling, hoped that his companion would not notice. 'I've only got one stubble field, which is the one on the photograph. There are no markings here. I guess it must be a hoax, somebody trying to make a fast buck, like you said.'

Weale studied his picture, compared it with the landscape, shook his head in bewilderment. 'It's the right field, sure enough,' his voice took on an angry tone, 'and there's sod all there. Christ, just wait till I get hold of that photographer!'

But Dick was not listening. A movement amidst the grazing sheep caught his eye, an animal that was white in colour, larger; had horns. . . Its head came up, it had recognized his voice, was beginning to canter towards him up the steep incline, full udder swinging.

'Gubbins! It's Gubbins!'

Tim Weale was already on his way back to his parked car in the farmyard. He wasn't interested in sheep or whatever animals these bumpkins kept. Right now his only concern was to phone his office, report that the whole thing was a fake, a hoax.

Dick dared not believe that the onrushing goat was the missing Gubbins until his fingers were stroking her smooth hair. She still wore her collar and he grabbed it, just in case she might suddenly disappear again.

'Where on earth have you been to, old girl?' She was pulling him along in her eagerness to get to the milking parlour. There was no mistaking the relief in her continual bleating, her eagerness for a bucket of concentrates. Wherever she had been, it was all forgotten. Suffice that she was home; nothing else mattered.

Ten minutes later Dick was squirting the milk from her teats, foaming it into the stainless steel bucket. There was no sign of mastitis, no discomfort as he squeezed. It was obvious that Gubbins had been milked regularly during her absence. He shook his head, made no attempt to understand for it was beyond his ken. As Jonjo had forecast, she had returned with the first frost.

Only then was he aware that the Land Rover was missing from the yard, and that there was no sign of either Brenda or Avis. He checked to ensure that Ben was still asleep in his room. Maybe Brenda had taken Avis down to the doctor's surgery.

'I really don't think there's any point in going back to the farm, Avis,' Brenda hoped that Dr Gorman might suddenly appear. 'I mean, it's burned out, there's nothing to see. It won't be good for you.'

'I want to go!' Avis was determined. 'If you won't take me, then I'll walk.'

'All right,' Brenda conceded, 'but we're not stopping. Just a quick look. The firemen won't thank us for hanging around, we'll only be in their way.'

As she climbed into the Land Rover Brenda wondered who the fellow was who had arrived about twenty minutes ago, what he had come for. Obviously, Dick had taken him to see something, not that there was anything to see. Maybe he was a detective just checking that Will Pocklington or Sharon Deeps wasn't hiding somewhere on the traditional farm. Or an insurance assessor jumping the gun. No, the latter usually took their time in coming to look. It was probably something quite innocuous and time-wasting.

The roof had collapsed on the Pocklingtons' farmhouse, a blackened, stonework skeleton that breathed smoke out of its many orifices through which firemen still played their hoses. The fire had travelled through the yard, taken the hay barns on its way to the small council estate two fields away. Only the potato field had slowed its progress, enabled the hoses to check its rampage of fiery destruction.

Avis stared out of the Land Rover, her eyes glazed, did not seem to understand. Or to care. This place meant nothing to her now; she was glad it was gone. Only her anguished memories were left.

'We'd better not stay long.' Brenda had deliberately left the engine running. 'Maybe after the fire's been put out you can come back and. . .'

'*Look!*' Avis screeched, pointed.

Brenda Kirby started, convinced that her worst fears were confirmed, that the sight of her burned-out home had snapped the other's mind.

'It's all right, Avis,' it clearly wasn't, 'they're just firemen. . .'

'Oh, *look*!' Avis fumbled the catch on the passenger door, almost fell into the yard. Brenda's restraining hand was pushed roughly away.

That was when Brenda looked, felt her senses begin to swim. It had to be an hallucination, some kind of cruel mirage induced by smoke inhalation, perhaps exhaustion. From the doorway of the grain store, the only building that had survived the blaze because of its steel construction, a young boy walked casually, aimlessly, kicked at a loose pebble and sent it spinning. Hands in the pockets of his jeans, his checked shirt looking as though it had been put on clean only that morning, he strolled in the direction of the parked Land Rover.

And there was no possible doubt in Brenda Kirby's mind that it was Will Pocklington, seemingly unconcerned at the devastation around him.

'Will! Oh, my poor baby!' Avis ran forward, clasped her son to her, held him tightly. 'Will, wherever have you been?'

He looked up, bewildered. 'Nowhere, Mum. Just around. What started the fire?'

'But you. . . oh, never mind.' Avis was crying now, her wet cheek pressed against her son's face. 'You can tell me all about it later. We're going back to the Kirbys' now. And I'm really glad our nasty old farm has been burned down.'

'I was just up the fields when I smelled the smoke,' Will said as his mother lifted him up into the cab of the Land Rover. 'You remember, Mum, I'd just gone for a walk. . .'

Brenda swung the vehicle round in a U-turn, headed back down the uneven track. A lot of questions were going to be asked but she doubted whether anybody would have the answers. Which was, perhaps, just as well. There were some things in life that it was preferable not to know.

'I think you ought to try to get some sleep.' John Deeps spoke from the doorway of the lounge, knew that his advice would go unheeded. It was just that he felt he had to say something, to break the long silence if for no other reason.

'I'm staying right here,' Fiona answered stubbornly, the way she had yesterday, and the day before. 'The phone might ring.'

Dr Gorman had sedated her but it had seemed to make little difference. Sometimes she dozed, awoke with a start, stared at the telephone by her elbow, willing it to ring. We've found her, Mrs Deeps. I'm afraid she's dead, though. Only grief would break the spell that held her in its fearful grip; the uncertainty that was destroying her slowly, day by day.

'She's dead, John.' And it's all your fault because you overruled me and let her go to the disco.

'We don't know that for sure.'

'*I* do.'

He sighed. There was no point in arguing. Sharon *was* dead, there could be no possible doubt about that. 'There was a big fire last night on the fields at the other end of the village. A couple of houses were gutted after it got out of control.'

'Oh.' Not even surprise. She didn't care, wouldn't even if their own house had been burned down. As it was, the house stank of burning, but

Fiona had not even noticed. She just stared at the phone, her eyes black-ringed, her features a whiter shade of pale.

John moved into the room, resisted the temptation to slip an arm round her to comfort her. She would have pushed him away: that was how it was between them, Sharon or no Sharon. The uncertainty was all that was holding them together; when the news finally broke, good or bad, that was it. Finis.

He had made up his mind to tell her before Sharon went missing, psyched himself up for it. Look, Fiona, our relationship is a sham, has been for the last two or three years, possibly longer. We stayed together for Sharon's sake, but she's big enough now, she doesn't care, anyway. No, I'm not going to run off, abandon you. And there isn't anybody else. I don't want anybody else. All I want to do is to work. I'm going to get an apartment in the city. Don't worry, I'll pay all your bills just like I always have, and I'll come here frequently. That way we'll see how a break works. It might even bring us together again.

He had rehearsed his speech aloud to himself in the privacy of his study; worked on it, perfected it. The break wouldn't bring them together again, that was the last thing he wanted. Fiona didn't want it, either, if she was honest with herself. Sharon wouldn't care a toss. So all three of them were getting what they wanted.

Only Sharon had gone and ruined it all. Later, much later, after they found the body, he would tell Fiona. For the moment, though, they had no choice but to stick together.

'There was a hard frost last night.' He moved to the window, looked out. He wasn't sure whether or not there was a fog mingling with the smoke haze. It didn't really matter.

'That busker's got her.' Fiona spoke expressionlessly, just a statement of fact, not even a hint of malice. 'I *know* it's him.'

'That's nonsense. The police checked him out. He's a harmless freak.'

'I could tell by her expression that day I saw her listening to him. She was infatuated with him. She didn't go to the disco, she went looking for him.'

There was no point in arguing; they had been through all that a score of times.

The doorbell rang, a soft resonant tone. Just once.

'There's somebody at the door, John.'

He tensed. The bad news, in all probability, wouldn't be relayed by phone. The police would call, a senior officer, break it gently. Probably Dr Gorman would come as well. John Deeps was afraid to answer the ring.

It rang a second time, and you sensed the impatience of whoever was standing out there on the step.

'Aren't you going to answer it, John?'

He moved, slow uncertain steps, hoping that perhaps whoever it was would get fed up with waiting and go away. Fiona seemed to be in some kind of a trance again, her eyes glazed as if she had cataracts, leaning forward in her chair because she was having difficulty in seeing the telephone.

He made it out into the hallway, hung back. He could see a silhouette through the bottle-glass window in the front door, a distorted, unrecognizable outline.

The doorbell rang again.

All right, I'm coming. Everybody was just too bloody impatient these days. He fumbled the Yale, clicked it back at the second attempt and opened the door a foot or so. Smoke wafted inside, smarted his eyes, made him cough so that he was unprepared for having the door pushed out of his grasp, the caller shoving her way inside.

'Hey, just a. . .'

'What kept you, Dad? Just got up, I suppose!'

Sharon stood there in the hall, as outrageously dressed as that night she had gone to the disco, her features white and strained as though she had not slept since.

'Where the hell've you been?' The words slipped out, the same as they would have done if she had come home the next morning instead of now. Instinctively angry, unable to comprehend, subconsciously trying to pretend that she had not been missing for more than a few hours. Because that was the only way that he could keep his sanity.

He heard Fiona getting up out of her chair in a rush, anticipated an hysterical scream, a tearful reunion. Her footsteps faltered; there was no cry of surprise or disbelief. Only an agonizing silence. Followed by a *thump* as she hit the white shag pile carpet and lay motionless.

CHAPTER NINETEEN

It was mid-morning before the sun finally penetrated the lingering mist and began to melt the frost on the fields and hedgerows. A stiff breeze sprang up, dispersed the smoke pall which hung over the village. For a few more hours the Indian summer would enjoy a final fling. By nightfall, the weather forecasters predicted, an area of low pressure would arrive from the Atlantic and rain and gales would spread across the whole of Britain.

Gubbins seemed quite content to remain in the goatshed with Abby. Dick filled the hayracks, topped up the water buckets; perhaps tomorrow he would put the goats out to graze. He might tether them.

News had just reached him, via Dr Gorman who had arrived to check on Avis and Will, that Sharon Deeps had also arrived home. Jonjo's predictions had come true. Dick was not altogether surprised.

For the second time that morning Dick Kirby walked up to the stubble field. He had nothing particular in mind today except routine chores; he would not be able to settle to anything else. He sensed a change in the atmosphere, not just the weather but a kind of widespread relief. The sheep grazed the clover between the corn stubble; they showed no signs of alarm at his approach. Whatever it was that had been making them tense these past weeks was gone.

Patches of frost still remained in the shade, beneath the hedges and under trees; leaves were falling with an urgency, as though they had to make up for the time lost during the late unseasonable climatic conditions. The gallinis were by the hedge at the far end of the pasture, clamouring their *get-back, get-back* to one another; they had relished a day's gleaning on Pocklington's stubble, and the sight of the charred and smoking acres frustrated and angered them. Now they would probably have to content themselves with searching for insects in the grass.

Dick checked to make sure that the corn rings really had disappeared, that it was not some trick played by the early morning mist and smoke haze. He walked down the steep slope and back up again; there was no evidence to suggest that anything untoward had disturbed the ground.

It was then that his eye caught the figure sitting in the far hedgerow. It was Jonjo, of course; even from this distance there was no mistaking the khaki denims, the hat tilted down over the bearded features, legs straight out in front of him, back resting against a hawthorn trunk. The busker had passed the night there, obviously, chosen a sheltered place in the thorny hedge, rejected the warmth and shelter of an outbuilding in preference to the open fields. Maybe he had slept through the stubble fire, aware of it yet accepting it, claiming that it was none of his business. Johnny Mack would carry the blame and he would never be able to defend himself because he had paid the price of his folly in failing to allow for even a brief change of wind direction; an eddying of the night breeze had been enough to bring about his own death.

Dick changed direction, began to walk towards the sleeping man. There were questions he wanted to ask him but he would not, because the answers would not be forthcoming. If Jonjo knew where Sharon and Will had been, Gubbins, too, he would not tell. Suffice that they had been taken by the angry forces of Nature venting their wrath over an environment that was being abused to the point of destruction. A warning, some would say; others would ridicule the suggestion. An agrochemist's daughter had been taken because her father devised and marketed harmful insecticides and pesticides; a farmer's son because his father had taken a sadistic delight in abusing the land. Worse, he had instigated that stubble fire, even after his death, a final legacy that had driven the mysterious corn creatures to destroy the home of his widow and son. In their uncontrollable fury, they had attempted to annihilate the village and its inhabitants.

But the frost had intervened at the eleventh hour, had spared human lives and further destruction.

There had been mistakes, too. The verger's death, doubtless, had not been intended; his weak heart had simply failed to stand up to the shock of the destruction of the Gospels before his eyes. Nature's memory was long; she had not forgotten the slaughter of her charges over a thousand years ago so that mankind could inscribe his own conceited history upon their skins. Maybe the Corn Goat had razed the village church to the ground in a moment of impetuosity because man had gathered there to give thanks for a harvest that had been grown and gathered in at the expense of the land, taking but putting nothing back except poisonous chemicals until the soil would eventually revert to a barren wilderness.

One could only guess, Dick reflected. Only Jonjo really knew, and he would not reveal his secrets.

The farmer stood there looking down on the busker. Frost sparkled on the soiled denims, glittered like cake icing on the shaggy beard. Jonjo did not move, slept heavily, completely unaware of Dick's presence.

'Hey, Jonjo, wake up, it's. . .'

Dick's outstretched foot was about to nudge the other awake but some sixth sense stopped it only inches from the busker's scuffed boot, left him precariously balanced. He dropped to one knee, and, with fingers that shook slightly, gently lifted Jonjo's frosted hat. The eyes beneath were closed, and the features had aged yet another decade since Dick had last looked upon them, wrinkled skin, lips sucked inwards over gums that might have been toothless. Wisps of corn straw adhered to the shock of greying hair. So peaceful, and yet it was a slumber from which Jonjo would never awaken. The first frost had come and Nature had reclaimed her own.

Dick pulled the hat down over Jonjo's face, straightened up, stood there with bowed head, his eyes suddenly misty; it might just have been from the stubble smoke that still drifted in the wind. Slowly he turned away, began the long walk back to the farmyard. There was a lot to be done between now and the spring, traditional farming methods to be resurrected so that people might watch and understand why progress was not always to the benefit of mankind.

Before it was too late. Jonjo's warning must not go unheeded. There was still time.

GUY N. SMITH FAN CLUB

Sheringham
West Street
Knighton
Powys LD7 1EN
Organiser: Sandra Sharp

Annual	(UK): £15.00	(USA): $30.00
Life	(UK): £35.00	(USA): $65.00

- Free subscription to *Graveyard Rendezvous* (the Guy N. Smith fanzine), the magazine for fans and aspiring writers
- Automatic invitations to launch parties
- Club events
- 10% discount on Guy N. Smith books by mail order
- Signed books
- T-shirts
- USA & foreign editions

The Lichfield Prize

the novel writing competition for aspiring authors

The Lichfield Prize could be the writing
opportunity you've been waiting for.

Now in its sixth competition year, the Lichfield Prize
literary competition offers the winning author the chance
to have their novel published by Hodder & Stoughton
and to receive £5000 in cash.

To follow in the footsteps of the competition's
previous winners you need to write a novel with
wide audience appeal and a story line based clearly
in Lichfield District in Staffordshire.

With a rich literary heritage, Lichfield District
provides a wealth of inspiration to authors.

The Lichfield Prize is held every two years.

Write for your Entrants Pack to:

Lichfield Prize (GS),
Information Centre, Donegal House, Bore Street,
Lichfield, Staffordshire WS13 6NE
or call: 01543 412047

The Lichfield Prize is currently promoted by
Lichfield District Council in association with

James Redshaw Ltd
Booksellers

and

Hodder & Stoughton
Publishers

143